LEAVING YOU

Cloudberry Inn Series #3

Karice Bolton

DEDICATION

To My Family. You are everything.

Chapter One

Lana

Lars Stockton was presumed dead. I remembered the last thing he'd ever told me. It was a simple couple of sentences, but he was a simple guy. His words got the point across, really.

Later, baby. It was good.

Just the simple act of remembering Lars telling me those words made an involuntary eye roll happen that I'd always wished I could have done in front of him. My reaction was silly, really. Everything happened a long time ago. Why did I care?

I looked toward the colorful gardens where my two sisters were laughing as their significant others wandered over and handed them the fresh lemonade I'd just put out on the deck.

The air was sweet with honeysuckle, and daisies erupted along the new perennial garden leading away from the inn. The world continued to spin. Life continued to move forward in the trajectory that had been set long ago.

But I knew I should be feeling something from this news about Lars.

I shook my head. It was a funny thing. The lack of reaction that those words produced was far more profound than hearing of his death. None of it really mattered, though. Everything happened a million years ago, and now he was presumed dead.

Might I add that, of course, Lars didn't just die? He had to leave that part of his life hanging too. Was he dead, or was he not dead? Why could the man never give any definite answers? Whether it was in his life or in his death, the guy seriously couldn't commit to anything—not even dying.

Which then made me seem like an awful person for remembering what a jerk he had been rather than mourning a life cut far too short. I had to get back on track.

My phone buzzed in my pocket, but I didn't want to look. It was as if that would make the news official, whatever it might be.

Life was okay.

No, life was good.

It was good, as Lars liked to tell his stable of girls back in high school. Another eye roll popped out of nowhere.

Apart from hearing about Lars this morning, I could say today wasn't just a good day. It was a great day, but I didn't want to sound like I had a heart of stone. Quite the opposite was true. My heart was as tender as a rose petal left in the sun for too long. It could shatter with the softest of touches or no touch at all. Just a gentle breeze could blow it away into a million little pieces.

I'd like to blame Lars for that, but I wasn't entirely

sure it was his fault.

What made today spectacular was that our family was slowly coming back together in a healthy way.

I could finally admit that it was fantastic having my sister Samantha back in Washington to help run the inn. Somehow, this wonder woman of a sister could manage to write bestselling books while operating the inn with me.

I glanced at my other sister, Vera, and smiled. I could also secretly confess to *no one in particular* how nice it was that Vera had opened a thriving bookstore in the mountains far away from Cloudberry. She was a much happier person for it, which in turn made me much more optimistic. It was my optimal state.

My head still spun from last autumn when I found out that I had a half sister named Charlotte in town. She had been Vera's best friend for much of their lives. Once the secret had been spilled, pieces of the puzzle began to fit. All the revelations had slowly highlighted that the perfect childhood I'd thought I'd had wasn't quite so perfect, after all.

It was an adjustment, to say the least.

4

My dad was still in the dark while we daughters grappled with who my parents pretended to be versus who they really were.

So, did the news this morning about Lars actually change the little part of the world I lived in?

Probably not.

Obviously, I felt terrible for his family and loved ones, but I didn't know him as the man he grew into. I just knew the teenage heartthrob he had been.

The phone now buzzed incessantly in my pocket, so I slipped it out to look at who was sending an onslaught of texts. I reached for my own glass of lemonade and glanced down at the screen. It was a friend from high school I'd only recently reconnected with when she stayed at Cloudberry Inn a few months back.

I eyed the phone screen that lit up with multiple messages.

Have you heard?
Can you believe it?
He was so young.

Didn't you date him?

My stomach tightened at the last message as I unlocked my phone and scanned the notes from Terry until I found the one that laid it all out.

They think Lars flew off his bike, but after this many days of searching the ravine, they're calling off the search. There's a memorial in Montana. They think his body floated down the river.

A shudder fluttered through me at the morbid thought.

Lars Stockton.

It was odd. I hadn't thought about him for years. He was my one attempt at rebelling as a teenager. Lars was the boyfriend all fathers in the world wanted to clobber as he rode away with their daughter into the sunset on his barely functioning motorcycle.

I touched my chest as the words settled around me.

Lars was no longer roaming the earth. He was my age, and life had been ripped out from under him.

It could happen to any one of us.

Drawing a breath, I looked toward the garden. I shook my head as I watched my sisters walking the gardens, holding hands with their spouses, and enjoying the carefree wonderland that Cloudberry Inn had always provided for brief spells.

I could stare out onto the property from any of the rooms in Cloudberry Inn and pretend what happened outside the walls never affected me. Good news or bad news, all I needed to do was focus on maintaining the inn.

But I'd be lying to myself.

Life was quite fragile. I'd already felt that the moment our mom was stolen from us far too young.

Yet, hearing that someone from high school had died in an accident, someone I'd shared all my firsts with, suddenly planted something deep inside me.

I turned to look at the place I'd called home for forever.

Cloudberry Inn was our legacy. I'd grown up here.

I took it over with my sisters after my mom's death when my dad fled to Arizona.

But was this where I wanted to die?

The rather macabre thought didn't send a shudder through me. Instead, a sneaky curiosity started to rear its ugly head.

I'd always been the happy and optimistic sister. Oddly, the thought of death never scared me. I didn't want others to pass away, but I never worried about it for myself. My family always thought my optimism was based in a wonderland of naiveté, but I knew enough about reality to plaster a smile on my face no matter the circumstance and just plow forward.

The one thing I excelled at in life was sticking my foot in my mouth. So recently, I'd been working on letting the words simmer in my mind for a few seconds before speaking. Sometimes it worked, and other times it didn't.

I was sure that my sisters had found their happiness, but the funny thing was that I never thought of myself as unhappy. I was content to work at Cloudberry forever.

Except on those rare occasions, if I really listened closely to my heart, the mere mention of staying forever made the beating muscle behind my chest sputter.

I thought about sharing the news from today.

If I wandered down to my sisters and told them about Lars, they'd make way too big of a deal about Lars's death and try to make it into something it wasn't. I hadn't spoken to him since high school. Once he'd taken up with my best friend right *after* he'd hit the ball out of the ballpark with me, I didn't really have much to say to either of them.

I certainly did not have feelings for him, and I didn't want my sisters to turn the truth into salty taffy. Once taffy was overstretched, the strings of sugar were never the same, and we'd come a long way. We didn't need to go backward.

I solidly remembered my time with Lars and didn't want my sisters to romanticize it. Lars, as a first, was less than ideal, but it didn't matter now. The poor guy was now toes up somewhere.

I let out a long sigh and wandered over to the

dripping wisteria, where the deep violet blooms stretched along the gazebo. The vine had long since bloomed, but a few blossoms were clinging to life, daring themselves to make it until the hot days of summer appeared.

As I thought about that last thought, I frowned. Was I just daring myself to make it to the next season? The next stage in life? Hearing the news early this morning started to marginally untwist the cork in me as I looked around the property. Thoughts had slowly begun leaking out, churning into questions and giving me no answers.

Shrugging to myself, I took a sip of lemonade and walked over to join my sisters.

Samantha's brown eyes caught mine, and she studied me. This was the fun part of being sisters with a writer. She could read my expressions more clearly than I could think them. Unfortunately, the skill could become exhausting at its best and downright infuriating at its worst.

"What's going on?" Samantha asked, dropping her husband's hand. Garrett's brows rose as he took a sip of lemonade. He seemed intrigued to hear the answer as well.

Even though the dynamics over the years between us sisters had been complicated, sticky, and as up and down as a rollercoaster ride, the men Samantha and Vera found knew how to navigate the waters between us better than we did.

I crossed my arms over my chest, which only highlighted my slender frame even more. Somehow, Samantha was the lucky one to have curves in all the right places and soft brown eyes that always looked as if she cared.

Lucky me looked like a dried-up sunflower most days, with a poof of brown hair sticking out of my messy bun and a stem for a body with a couple of floppy arms to complete the gangly look. And my green eyes? They were the murky color of a swamp that someone would expect the Loch Ness monster to pop up from. To this day, I wasn't sure my eyes were genuinely green.

I eyed Vera, who took after me a little more than Samantha when it came to body type, and she was staring right at me too.

"Come on, Lana," Samantha tried again. "You look like someone died."

My eyes widened, and Samantha's hands slipped to her mouth while Vera snorted.

Vera always had a knack.

"Oh, no." Vera shook her head. "Someone did die?"

A huge sigh escaped my lips, and I nodded. "Lars Stockton."

"Why is that name familiar?" Vera asked, glancing at Samantha.

Truth be told, Vera was the older sister and very infatuated with the man now standing beside her, so it's no surprise that she didn't remember a thing about my first boyfriend.

"He was her..." Samantha looked at the two guys as if she wanted to be discreet, but there wasn't a discreet bone in her body. "First time. First everything, right?"

My cheeks reddened, and I laughed. "Yes, thank you for that brief highlight reel."

"Oh, geez," Garrett said softly. "I'm really sorry."

Vera's husband, Drew, shook his head. "Wow. Me too. What a shock."

I nodded and suddenly had diarrhea of the mouth. "It's totally fine. I hadn't kept in touch. He was kind of a dirtbag. Slept with a lot of girls in high school, including my best friend." I shrugged and then suddenly realized what it sounded like. "And let me just say she was no longer my best friend after that."

Eek! Why couldn't I stop?

Shaking my head frantically, I touched my forehead and groaned. "That's not what I meant to say at all. I'm sure he grew out of his bad habits." I glanced at Drew and grimaced. "I was trying to say that it's not a relationship like you have with my sister. There's not that history and connection and wondering *What if?* for all these years. He kind of left a sour flavor. But as a man, I'm sure he changed, and I'm heartbroken for his family."

Could I sound like I was any worse of a human being? A man just died, and I was somehow preaching about all of his bad habits? Maybe I really shouldn't leave the safety of the inn.

Samantha and Vera laughed and nodded.

"Lars was probably the worst possible guy to date in high school." Samantha nodded. "Even though I wasn't home much during that time, the things I remember were pretty awful." She glanced around and added. "May he rest in peace."

Vera snickered. "Sorry. This isn't funny." She glanced at Drew, who smiled at her as if she were the queen herself.

"No, it's probably not," I confirmed, smiling at the lovebirds. I'd say it was just a phase between these two, but they were meant for one another.

Samantha pointed at me. "Remember the day after you two slept together for the first time? He took you to the tulip festival and left you stranded in one of the fields while he took off with one of his buddies on his motorcycle? You had to walk home."

I laughed. "Why, yes. I do. Thank you for bringing that up." My head cocked slightly as I studied my sister. "How did you know about that?"

I had been so mortified that I never told a soul.

Samantha blushed. "I read your diary."

"You did not." I couldn't remember for the life of me what I'd written in it, but I bet it was more than I'd want my kid sister to know.

She nodded. "I did."

"You're such a writer." I groaned and shook my head as my phone buzzed again, and I read the message, paraphrasing aloud. "Sounds like Lars had moved to Montana a few years back. Anyway, he veered off a sharp turn in the middle of the night. The bike went one direction, and he went the other, or so they think. They haven't found his body." I scanned the last of the message. "But they are presuming him dead. They think his body might have gotten swept down the river. Yikes." I shook my head. "They're holding a memorial on Saturday."

"They're having a memorial when they haven't found his body?" Samantha asked.

I nodded. "Sounds like it."

I bit my tongue so I didn't add my one-liner about his lack of commitment I'd come up with earlier.

"You know, this might sound crazy, but I think I'm

going to go to his memorial."

Samantha and Vera both looked surprised, but they nodded in agreement.

"I think that's a great idea," Samantha said. "Get some time away. You haven't had a vacation for years."

I laughed. "Yes, nothing better than a funeral for a break."

CHAPTER TWO

Jacob

I stared at Ted, my manager, who was less than pleased with my recent decision to forgo a tour next year. Of course, if he knew what I was really thinking, he'd probably jump off the Golden Gate Bridge.

I was done. D-O-N-E.

I'd been on the road touring since I was seventeen. First, I was in a boy band I'd rather not remember, and then my solo album took off. With over a decade of hits, I was positive I hadn't been in my own home in San Francisco for more than forty days of the last three hundred and sixty-five.

As far as the house in Montana that was supposed to be my escape? I fled there once for six consecutive days.

"I'm headed to Big Fork," I stated without any hesitation.

"For how long?" Ted's eyebrows turned pointy as he stared at me.

"Long enough to know I might as well sell this place." I tapped the couch my arms were stretched out on. My knee bobbed as I waited for Ted to say something, but I think he knew.

He knew if he said the wrong thing, I'd dig my heels in and never record again.

Little did he know, I'd already made that decision.

Ted eyed the woman on my balcony. "Who's she?"

My stomach knotted.

Her name was Delila, and I'd been the sucker who fell for her story until I started realizing the story constantly changed depending on the audience. I knew her Instagram was about as phony as her real life, but I indeed recognized my house in a lot of her posts.

In fact, her words had metamorphosized into such a different tale from when I first met her that I couldn't even remember fact from fiction.

What I did know was that she liked it when I wasn't at my house and preferred the pool boy, who'd barely turned twenty-one.

"Met her about six months ago." Which translated into seeing her maybe three or four times. "We hit it off."

Ted's brows flattened. "So, she's the reason you're not going to tour next year, Jacob Miller?"

"Nope."

"She's going with you to Big Fork?" he prodded.

I shook my head and clasped my hands together. "Nope."

"Does she know that?"

I laughed and slid my hands through my hair and sighed. "Ted, I don't even think she knows my birthday, let alone that I have another house in Montana."

"Then why's she here?"

"She said her place was getting renovated. Hook,

line, and sinker, I fell for it." I shrugged.

Ted shook his head. "I think you're making a huge mistake."

I leaned forward and propped my elbows on my knees. "Do you know what it means to be uninspired?"

"Of course."

I nodded. "When you're a songwriter, it's a bad thing."

"Good. So, you just need a little time away, and all will be better." He flashed his pearly whites in my direction, and my stomach dipped.

This was precisely what I'd hated about the entertainment industry. It was as if the people getting paid by you or paying you felt as if they had some sort of hold on you and had the right to tell you what was best for your life, your livelihood.

I shook my head. "I don't know, Ted. We'll have to see. I'm not going to write songs I don't want to write. I'm not going to sing songs I don't care about. I did that once."

Ted's eyes lit up. "But look where it got you." He

waved his hands around.

My brows arched. "Yeah. Let's take a closer look at that. I'm sitting in a home that I own but don't actually live in, and I couldn't even find an extra roll of toilet paper if my life depended on it. I have a woman whom I invited into my home to stay because I am so utterly lonely that the thought of coming home to a stranger was better than coming home to no one. I'm busy paying everyone else's salaries to the detriment of my own mental health." I shook my head and let out a sigh.

Ted stood firm. "You're not a sellout. You make good music."

I scowled. "Thanks, Ted. I hadn't thought of myself as one until you brought it up."

"You know what I mean. You write good music."

"Yeah, I know." I stood and walked over to the bland, mammoth kitchen that had about as much personality as the woman on the balcony. I grabbed some water and took a sip. "And I want to keep it that way. I don't want to sing lyrics generated to get a bunch of screaming teenage girls flashing their braces at me." I shook my head. "I write my own stuff because I feel it. Those words circle in me and sing out of me because they are part of me. They're precious to me."

I knew Ted wanted to roll his eyes so badly it hurt. He didn't care about the artist or the energy it took to create. Instead, he cared about the percentage dropping into his bank account. But he was good at what he did, so I only tortured him now and again.

"What are you really telling me?" Ted's focus sharpened as he watched me sip the water.

"I'm telling you that I need a break. This next year, I'll be in Montana." I shrugged. "I don't know what will come of it."

"You'll be writing music, though." Ted didn't bother to phrase it as a question.

"I don't know what I'll be doing, Ted. I might. I might not."

"What if I told you *what* to write? What the people want to hear? I scour your socials all the time. I could give you a theme or—"

I laughed. "You're not getting the message."

"No, I guess I'm not."

"I want to be inspired." I smiled, knowing the words coming out of my mouth would teach him nothing. "I want to feel the words pouring out of me and feel energized at the end, not drained, not miserable."

"You're miserable?" he asked.

I nodded. "I'm on the edge, Ted."

"There are things for that."

My eyes widened. "Seriously?"

"I'm kidding."

I knew he wasn't, which was what made this decision even easier.

"I'm headed to Montana. I'm selling this place." Just saying the words made me feel better.

"What about her?" Ted asked, glancing at the balcony.

"I'll let her know."

"You're an enigma." Ted sighed and shook his head. "Or a cliché."

I grinned and nodded. "I'm probably both." I walked over to Ted. "And I don't care."

He nodded.

"I think that's the problem right there. I've stopped caring." I looked around the bare room. "There's nothing here for me."

There really wasn't anything for me in Montana, either, aside from the solitude I desperately craved, but it was a start.

"Don't you worry about waking up one day, realizing you're old enough to collect social security, and yet you've never found that person to share your life with?" I asked.

Ted looked painfully disappointed. "I don't give it an ounce of thought. Most men would love to be in your shoes, Jacob." He shoved his hands into his jeans like a scolded toddler. "I just don't get what's come over you. This isn't the Jacob I know." He pointed toward the balcony. "Having a woman move in who you barely know? Now *that's* the Jacob I know."

Talking to Ted about anything somewhat philosophical would be about as pleasant as chatting with a cinderblock wall.

"What do you want me to tell the press?" he asked, looking agitated.

"How about nothing? They won't notice. There are enough insta-celebrities and social media influencers to draw their attention." I threw my hands in the air. "No leaks needed. Just a peaceful exit to paradise."

"I don't like how this is sounding." Ted paced in front of the fireplace.

"I'm sorry about that."

This whole discussion came as a shock to Ted, no doubt. But it needed to happen.

"What do you think is going to happen if you just disappear and come out on the other end with no music?"

I shrugged, seeing the shark come out of Ted.

"I'll tell you what's going to happen. Nothing. There will be two others ready to take your place."

"It is what it is, Ted. I can't force it any longer." I glanced at Delila on the balcony, watching her filming herself for her socials.

"I can see your mind is made up. When are you leaving?" Ted asked, realizing there wasn't a thing he could do or say to convince me to stay.

"It is." I grimaced. "As soon as I can."

Ted let out a defeated sigh and nodded.

Ted walked over and gave me a hug. "I just hope this isn't career suicide."

I didn't have the heart to tell him that I didn't care if it was.

"I'll let myself out."

I smiled, feeling a burst of energy. The hard part was over.

Hearing my manager's footsteps echo down the hallway gave me a sense of finality to this decision.

Now, I just needed to let Delila in on my plans.

As I walked toward the balcony, she spun around and opened the gigantic sliding glass door.

"How are you, love?" she asked, clutching her phone.

I wasn't sure there had ever been a moment, not even a second, where she wasn't clinging to her lifeline of people praising her every sentence, smile, and prop.

"Good." I gave a stiff nod, wondering what had ever gotten into me to let her stay here. "Glad to be off the road."

Her smile curled at the edges as if she were debating how to let me down. Finally, she stepped inside and rested her hand on my chest.

She looked up at me with her brown eyes. "I'm absolutely slammed."

My brows perked up. "Yeah?"

She nodded and took a step back as her hand dropped to her side.

"I don't think I'll be very good company while you're back." She twisted her lips into a perfect pout. She was so used to knowing what facial expressions photographed best that I was never sure what the real Delila looked like at any given moment.

I feigned a scowl even though ecstasy was pumping through my veins. "That's too bad."

Delila nodded. "I'm actually planning to stay at a place with friends. It's freaking amazing on the hillside down near Malibu or somewhere. There's even an infinity pool. Great for pics."

"Ah." I nodded solemnly. "Going south."

I stayed still, trying to fight the urge to run to the

bedroom to help her pack.

"I'm sorry, love." She pretended to exaggerate her pout. "But my career is taking off, and I just can't miss this opportunity. A whole bunch of us will be living there, and it will be totally epic. We'll be trading stories and gaining each other's followers."

I smiled. "I get it. Opportunities like this only come once in a blue moon."

She nodded eagerly and walked over to the kitchen to grab a water. "Exactly. You're not mad?"

Hell, no! Could I buy you a plane ticket?

"Nah. I get it." I shut the slider and turned around to see her guzzling water. "When are you planning on heading out?"

"I think tomorrow. I want to make sure I get the good bedroom."

We were definitely in different solar systems.

She smiled and walked over to me. "I can see the disappointment in your eyes. I'm sorry."

I hid another smile and nodded. "It's for the best. I'm never in town. It's not fair to you."

Why did lyrics not roll off my lips as easily as this?

"I'll miss you," she cooed.

I was confident it was a coo. She'd do just fine down in Los Angeles. I could have asked her about her house she was waiting on or any number of stories I'd heard over the last six months, but what was the point? The crowd she and I ran in was built on mirages.

"Go have fun and rule the social media world." I winked, and I wasn't a winker.

She hopped on her toes and clapped her hands together with the phone inside.

"Okay. I'd better go pack. I'm not great with goodbyes." She wrinkled her nose and spun on her heels.

I smiled and watched her trundle down the hall to pack her belongings.

For the first time in years, I could breathe again.

CHAPTER THREE

Lana

The moment I'd hit Montana's state line, it was as if the sky had opened and someone had spilled a jar of cyan paint as far as the eye could see. The beauty was breathtaking, and the expansive views made it impossible not to feel as small as a ladybug as me and my economy-sized car sped along the eighty-miles-an-hour interstate.

The only thing that would make this trip better would be if the destination weren't a funeral. The bright side was that it wasn't mine, but I probably shouldn't be bragging about that. I'd always had a bad habit of looking on the bright side of life. This condition had gotten me in trouble with school, with my family, with my job at the inn... with the world, really.

I'd heard people call me plastic, phony, and fake, but the truth was that I just wanted to be liked, to be happy, and to be in my own bubble.

Rather than admit I might have a few faults or there might be danger lurking ahead, I tended to put my head down and push through. If money problems erupted at the inn, I'd forge ahead and pray that they'd resolve themselves, and most often, they did. If I'd made a bad decision, I didn't beat myself up. I just pressed forward and hoped the blow-up would resolve quickly. This line of thinking had always served a purpose for me.

I was a happy person.

If I felt down, I'd remind myself to smile, and it worked.

Nine times out of ten, it worked.

But this last year, I'd noticed my technique had its faults. When Samantha came back to the inn to help, I had to admit to myself and the world around us that I needed help. I didn't excel at running the business side of the inn. The whole balancing cash flow with different things that crept up at the inn hadn't been my strong suit. The ideas and executions for making the inn a better destination went flawlessly for me. Coming up with the money to pay for it all? Not exactly my forte.

I gripped the steering wheel as my phone's navigation system interrupted Cindy Lauper's *Girls Just Want to Have Fun* over my car stereo, and I took a left toward the lodge. Cindy came back on, and I started belting out my best rendition.

Somewhere in Idaho, I'd decided that this song would be my motto. Again, probably not the sanest choice for a funeral, but this trip was about more than Lars's funeral.

It was about reminding myself that life existed beyond Cloudberry.

I knew my sisters were worried about my taking off for Montana by myself. It wasn't that I was incapable, but a road trip two states away was kind of out of the ordinary. I rarely left a ten-mile radius from Cloudberry, let alone decide to venture to Montana for an old high school boyfriend's funeral. Come to think of it, I think they were more worried about my state of mind than my actually arriving safely in Montana.

I'd left the inn this morning at a quarter to five, and so far, I'd only stopped for gas, which led me to stock up on every kind of chip, pepperoni, jerky, and energy drink I could find. My car looked like a hurricane had twirled around inside, but I could clean it up, and who really cared? It wasn't like I was trying to impress anyone.

As the lodge came into view, I smiled at the beauty and knew I'd made the right choice. I wanted to hear about the man Lars turned out to be, who he'd settled down with, and what his friends thought about him, and what better place than in Montana?

The lodge was the size of at least four Cloudberry Inns, and there were several smaller buildings nestled along the property, which looked onto a small lake. The setting was beautiful, and I hadn't even gotten out of my car. I quickly found a parking place near the lobby's sign, turned off the car, and just sat for a few minutes with my eyes closed.

I'd driven eight hours yesterday, overslept at a small motel this morning, and had been driving for another eight today. Granted, some of that was because I'd taken a wrong turn a time or two, but I'd made it in time for Lars's service tomorrow at the lodge.

Several shrieks interrupted my relaxation. I quickly peered out my window into the parking lot, where I saw a group of teenagers hopping up and down and spinning in circles. I searched the parking lot, and I didn't see anything that would get a scream out of me, but I was over thirty, so who knew?

I took it as my cue, climbed out of my car, and stretched toward the sky. A chill was already settling in the air as night traded for the day, and I couldn't wait to grab some dinner.

The warm glow inside the lobby made me smile. Was this the excitement that people felt when they drove up to Cloudberry Inn? An escape awaiting them? A refuge? I smiled at the thought and made my way toward the lobby when two more shrieks erupted from the group of girls and nearly made me run into the door.

I glanced behind me to see a man tugging on the brim of his cowboy hat a little more as he started toward the door in front of me.

Did all cowboys get this greeting in Montana?

His eyes were hidden by the brim of his hat, which forced me to catch a look at his lips. They weren't smiling, and they weren't frowning either, but they were awfully beautiful. I thought about how thin my lips were and wondered why men always got long lashes, full lips, and strong jawlines.

As I made it to the entry, a few of the girls came running up behind us, and he quickly grabbed for the door to hurry everything along. He reached over my head so I could move inside.

"After you, Ma'am." He tipped his hat with his free hand.

My blood froze as my body kept moving.

Ma'am? How had I gone from Miss to Ma'am?

When did this happen?

Shouldn't there be some sort of slow transition from one to the other? What made this *first* even worse was that he had the sexiest voice this side of the Mississippi. It was soothing and sensuous—and I couldn't believe I'd just been called Ma'am.

I glanced down at my grey joggers and pink tee with a plaid button-down tied around my waist. My blue sneakers completed the look, and I suddenly realized I might have earned that title.

"Thank you," I muttered, moving into the expansive lobby.

He gave a quick nod and beelined away from me with his teenagers right on his tail. I spotted a karaoke sign near the lounge he was headed to and smiled.

Maybe he was tonight's local act. I pursed my lips together at the thought of being called Ma'am again and headed toward the counter to check in.

"Good evening," a perky brunette chimed. "Checking in?"

I nodded. "Lana Roberts for two weeks."

The woman nodded and requested my credit

card and identification. "Any fun plans?"

I smiled and nodded. "I'm attending a funeral tomorrow."

The woman's eyes widened as she handed me back the cards. "I'm so sorry."

I shook my head and touched my forehead. "Sorry. I didn't mean that was the fun part. I plan on seeing the sights, enjoying the outdoors, all of that."

The woman nodded, sliding my keycard to me. "I'm sorry for your loss."

"Oh, thanks. It wasn't much of one. I hadn't seen him since high school."

The woman's brows rose as I groaned internally and snagged the cards, realizing I had a long way to go before my foot-in-mouth disease went away.

I nodded. "Thank you, though."

She grimaced and gave me directions to my room when I spotted the cowboy sitting at the bar with a drink.

He looked conflicted, uneasy, and like he wanted to run away. The teenage girls had disbanded, so I wasn't sure what he wanted to get away from.

Kind of like how I felt right now after insulting the dead.

I pointed toward the lounge. "Is he some local celebrity or something? He was being followed by a bunch of screaming girls."

The woman smiled. "Something like that."

"So, is he like the entertainment for tonight?"

She laughed. "It's karaoke night, but I highly doubt he'll be up there."

I nodded. "You have karaoke?"

"Once a week. The locals love it." She smiled. "You sing?"

I chuckled. "Only in my car or shower."

"Me too." She laughed as I walked away.

Karaoke. I hadn't sung Karaoke in eons, and that had been at someone's house. It sounded almost fun if I had a bit of liquid courage. Plus, the bar probably served good bar food.

By the time I'd grabbed my bags out of the car and found my room, newfound energy had thrust me forward. I didn't know if it was the promise of a cheeseburger or the prospect of seeing that cowboy again.

Either way, I'd showered, pulled on a black silk dress with spaghetti straps, gathered my hair into a slicked-back ponytail, and even managed to put on some lipstick.

Maybe he'd think twice about who he called Ma'am.

I grabbed my room key and slid it into my wallet before making my way down to the lounge. The lights had dimmed since when I'd first arrived at the hotel, and the small space was crowded with couples.

Scanning the bar, my heart dropped when I realized the cowboy wasn't here any longer. A sigh escaped my lips as I found a tiny table by the stage and sat down. A cute bartender with a beard came over instantly and spun a drink coaster in front of me.

"What can I get you?" His smile was warm and friendly, but his lips... his lips weren't like the cowboy's. Although, the bartender's mouth was a little hard to find under the beard.

"What's your special?" I asked, realizing it had been so long since I'd been out that I didn't even know what was popular.

He smiled and nodded. "I make a mean pink squirrel."

My brows rose. "Pink squirrel."

"It's like a milkshake for grownups."

"What's it taste like?"

"Chocolate and almond."

"Do you think it would go with a burger?" I asked.

He laughed. "What doesn't?"

"Good point. I'll take a pink squirrel."

The bartender nodded and slid a menu in front of me. "You plan on getting up tonight to belt out any tunes?"

"Only if multiple pink squirrels are involved."

"So, there's a chance."

I laughed and nodded. "It all rides on your drink-making abilities."

"The pressure's on." He grinned and nodded. "What brings you here?"

I thought back to my encounter at the check-in desk and decided to change my tactic.

"I'm here for a memorial service."

The bartender nodded solemnly. "Lars?"

"You know him?"

He shook his head. "I think just about every bartender in town knows him or knew him."

I couldn't hide my surprise and was grateful it wasn't me sticking my foot in my mouth. "Really?"

"That came out wrong," the bartender added.

I laughed. "Not really. The truth is the truth. My truth is that I last saw him in high school when he'd dumped me for my best friend right after he and I had slept together, but I thought this would be a good excuse for a getaway."

"Ah, the old funeral-excuse-for-a-vacation trick."

"You know it?"

He ran his fingers along his beard. "Used it myself, actually."

"Does it make us awful people?" I whispered.

I heard a snicker from behind and turned around to see the cowboy sitting at a table. Our eyes connected, and it felt like everything in the room dissolved into the Montana dirt. His brilliant blue eyes stayed on me for a beat too long as I squirmed in my chair. The bartender wandered away, but I couldn't pull my gaze off the stranger sitting only a few feet away.

But thanks to my lack of social skills when it mattered, I stared at him and blurted out one question.

"What's so funny?"

The question only made the cowboy smile wider.

He removed his hat and placed it on the chair next to him, which only made my heart squish a little harder. This man was drop-dead gorgeous.

Seeing him with the hat made my heart skip a beat. Seeing him without the cowboy hat made my heart thump wildly.

"The last ten seconds of your chat with the bartender sounded like an entire country song wrapped in a tidy little package."

I laughed. "It probably did sound that way, but I don't listen to country."

"You're in a beautiful lodge in the middle of Big Sky Country, and you don't listen to country?"

I shook my head. "No. I probably should. I'm

guessing I'd relate to the songs."

"Yeah?" His blue eyes bored into mine, and I found myself entranced. "Tell me more."

My tummy tightened into a million knots as I looked at this beautiful stranger.

Was I being hit on, or was he just nice?

I wiggled in my chair before turning it to face him easier as the bartender brought over the pink squirrel.

"You know more about me in the last thirty seconds than I do about you." I narrowed my eyes on him as I took a sip of the magical cocktail. The sweetness coated my lips. The drink was delicious. "Are you here on vacation?"

Hopefully, he wasn't Lars's best friend.

The sexy stranger tilted his head and nodded. "Kind of. I have a vacation home here."

I laughed and wiggled my brows. "Ooh, fancy."

He ran his fingers along his strong jawline and nodded. "I suppose it sounded a bit like an asshole statement."

I set my drink down. "Not at all. I can barely keep

one home tidy. I can't imagine trying to do two."

"Where's your other home?" I asked, taking another sip. I couldn't leave this drink alone.

"San Francisco, but I'm selling it," he added.

"So, technically, every single day will be a vacation for you." I glanced toward the stage where someone was setting up for the night's entertainment.

"I hope so."

The bartender brought the guy a drink and noticed mine was already half down. "Would you like another one?"

"It's like candy," I nearly whispered. "Yes, please."

The bartender smiled and wandered toward the bar as I turned to look at my cowboy.

"These could get me in big trouble." I shrugged. "But you only live once, right?"

"Something like that." He studied me, and every single cell in my body ignited. "Where are you from?"

I drew a breath. "I help run an inn with my sister back in Washington."

"Nice. That's a beautiful state."

I nodded. "It's very green. Although, in the summer, it's been more and more brown."

He shook his head. "I think that's everywhere."

"You gonna join us, Jacob?" A man stood on the stage staring right at my cowboy.

"I don't think so. I've had enough practice to last a lifetime."

The man nodded and scanned the bar, which was filling up pretty rapidly.

"You come here often, Jacob?" I asked, liking his name.

He looked like a Jacob. With his muscular physique, blue eyes, and sandy hair, the name Jacob fit him.

"Not too much, no." He glanced around the bar and put his cowboy hat back on.

My brow arched, and I laughed. "Worried you might run into a few exes around here?"

His lips parted, but he closed his mouth. "You found out my name. What's yours?"

"Lana." I smiled and took a deep breath. "Lana Roberts."

"Well, Lana. Do you mind if I take a seat with you?"

My cheeks flushed at the realization that this guy was actually flirting with me. The sexiest man in all of Montana wanted to share a table.

So, I had to do what I did best.

"I don't know." I scowled. "You called me *Ma'am* earlier, and I didn't think I'd already hit that age bracket. It carries a lot of responsibility, and I like to shy away from that."

He drew a breath and shook his head. "That was you?"

I glanced down at my dress and laughed. "I clean up nice, huh?"

Jacob laughed and shook his head. "It's not that. It wasn't you. I just registered a female in front of me, and I didn't think twice."

"Worried about the attack of the teenagers or something?" I teased.

"Actually, yeah. Teenage girls can be ruthless."

"You must sing karaoke more than you're letting on if you have that kind of reputation around here."

Jacob sat down and put his drink in front of him as the bartender delivered mine.

I thanked him and felt Jacob's gaze on me, which did all kinds of fun things to me. It had been so long since something like this had happened, I wanted to commit this feeling to memory.

"That guy was an idiot," Jacob said quietly.

I whipped my gaze to his. "I don't think so. He was just trying to keep my drink refilled."

Jacob chuckled. "No, the guy who dumped you."

"Technically, I wasn't dumped." I grinned. "He just stopped talking to me and moved on, but thank you. I like to think he missed out."

"Well, he's really missing out now." Jacob grimaced and took a drink.

I nodded and smiled, realizing it wasn't only me who had the foot-in-mouth disease. I shoved the empty glass aside and started on the next pink squirrel.

"I appreciate that," I said softly. "To be honest, I don't even know why I'm here."

"Closure?" he asked.

"I suppose, but I hadn't given this guy a thought since I found out he'd passed." I shrugged. "It just kind of jolted something inside me. I mean, I'm a happy camper wherever you stick me, but out of nowhere, this little worrisome feeling erupted, and I've been making impromptu decisions ever since."

Jacob nodded. "I'm sure the guy... what's his name?"

"Lars."

"I'm sure Lars would be happy to know that he's given the people he left behind a little something to think about."

I smiled. "Like live life to the fullest."

Jacob raised his glass, and I raised mine.

"To Lars," Jacob said.

"To Lars." My glass touched his as the lights dimmed. I took a sip of my pink squirrel and wondered if I'd just made a toast I'd regret.

CHAPTER FOUR

Jacob

Lana ordered another pink squirrel, and I watched her demeanor relax with each passing sip. Her beautiful brown hair scraped against her bare shoulders. Her infectious laugh garnered the attention of every male and female in the small bar. Her willowy figure made my mind go to places I hadn't visited in a very long time.

This woman was a kick in the pants. She was here for a funeral for a guy she barely knew, but she hadn't been damaged from her encounter with him. Instead, she rolled with the punches. She seemed to possess what I wanted.

The ability to be absolutely content with whatever life dealt her.

"Tell me what you're thinking," she said softly as her eyes connected with mine.

There was something about the way she looked at me that made me feel like I'd just won the lottery a million times over.

She could be chatting it up with the eager bartender, but she chose me.

"I'm thinking about how infectious your spirit is." I watched her for a reaction. There was being honest, and then there was being honest.

Her brows raised. "Really?"

I nodded. "You're so easygoing."

She chuckled. "I always thought I was kind of high-strung. Maybe it's the vacation." She glanced at her nearly empty glass. "Or the pink squirrels."

I grinned. "Could be."

Someone on the stage grabbed a microphone and announced the first singer.

It probably seemed odd that I wanted to give up

my career, yet I surrounded myself with music. I didn't even understand it, exactly, but the moment I'd heard about this place the first time I stayed at my place, I made a visit. The music, the amateur musicians, it all rang up home. These people loved the act of singing for the sake of nothing more than making music. Sure, some of them might need a belt or two of liquid courage to roll onto the stage and sing a tune or two, but the music pulled them to the stage.

I'd been missing that for years.

I glanced at Lana as the first song started. Her head started bopping as the singer started singing Pink Floyd's *Mother*.

The audience started cheering, and I knew I'd made the right decision to come here tonight, even if it meant running the risk of being recognized beyond the group of teenage girls. Sometimes, it was nice to just live.

The man singing gripped the microphone as if his life depended on it, and Lana just moved to the music, closing her eyes and living in the moment.

My eyes lowered to her lips, and I couldn't

imagine how great it would be to kiss her. She clapped her hands slowly as her head swayed, and it was the most beautiful moment I'd ever experienced, and I had no clue why.

As the riff started, Lana opened her eyes, and her gaze caught mine. She blushed and smiled as she shrugged.

"I'm a sucker for Pink Floyd. What can I say?"

I smiled, feeling like I was in my own version of heaven. "You don't have to say a thing."

She took another sip and swayed as the singer finished his song, and the crowd went wild. Lana stood and clapped her hardest as a timid woman got on stage.

The female singer was so slight and wouldn't look at the audience. She looked like a little mouse escaping with her cheese, head down, and determined to get off the stage as fast as she got there.

"You got this, girl," Lana hollered right as Lady Gaga's music erupted from the speakers. The hit *Applause* roared through the speaker, and this woman sang her heart out, channeling her inner Gaga, and I truly believe it was partly because Lana was jumping up and down as enthusiastically as any fan I'd ever encountered.

The singer raised her head as the confidence built and more people started dancing to her singing.

Seeing what Lana could do for a person without even thinking twice about it blew me away. The bartender brought over another pink squirrel, which Lana took a sip of between shaking her hips.

When the woman finished singing, she walked off the stage as if she owned the place. I looked over at Lana and knew that feeling washing over the singer was purely because of Lana. One glance from her, and you felt like a million bucks.

Lana took a seat and smiled. "I love Gaga, and that gal took it to a whole new level."

I nodded. "Me too."

Now probably wasn't the time to mention that Gaga was just as nice in person as she was an incredible singer.

The truth of this night was that I'd probably never see Lana again, and it was fun to pretend to not be me.

Her gaze connected with mine. "Are you going to get up there?"

Lana's question startled me. "No."

"Oh, come on." She patted my shoulder. "I bet you sing really well. You have a really sexy voice." She laughed as her gaze widened. "Oops. I've been trying to work on words just tumbling out."

I smiled. "Sexy voice, huh?"

"Like you didn't know." She looked around the room as the lull in singers quieted the bar. "So, what's the deal? You gonna get up there and sing your little heart out?"

"Nah." I shook my head. "It's not my thing."

Her brows shot up. "You think you're better than this?"

I threw my head back in laughter. "Not even in the slightest." I lowered my gaze to her. "What about you? Are you going to get up there?"

She shrugged and eyed her drink. "I've had three pink squirrels. I just might."

Hearing this revelation sent a thrill of excitement through me for no other reason than I wanted to hear the song that she'd pick to sing.

Would it be Gaga? Would it be Madonna? The Beatles? The Stones?

I smiled just thinking about it.

"What's got you smiling?" she asked, her eyes falling to my lips.

"You."

She chuckled and brushed her hair behind her shoulders. Her slender, bare shoulders begged to be kissed.

Man, this was hard.

"Are you always this smooth?" she asked.

I laughed and shook my head.

"Well, I'm flattered. I'm just going to sit here and pretend that you don't use those lines on all the women."

When I looked at Lana, I saw a vulnerable woman sitting in front of me, but her vulnerability was such an asset. In passing, she'd mention an insecurity and bolstered it up with a look that said otherwise.

"Do you even know how beautiful you are?" I asked, pressing my fingers together.

She looked around the bar and smiled. "The lights are low. You've been drinking. You're delirious with the energy running through this room." She winked at me.

Winked at me!

"But thank you." She polished off her third pink squirrel.

Lana stood up and wandered over to the bartender who was in charge of karaoke selection. His eyes cascaded down her slinky dress, and my hands fisted, which made me laugh to myself.

She wasn't mine. I couldn't claim her. I was acting ridiculous.

As if she could read my mind, she spun around, and our eyes connected.

My heart sputtered as I felt the strongest pull to a woman I'd ever felt.

Lana blew me a kiss, and I shook my head, knowing I was in trouble.

I sat back in the chair and took a drink of my gin as she wandered back to the table.

"Why do I feel like you're devising some devious

plan?" I asked, leaning into the table.

"Who, little old me?" She laughed, and I knew there was no going back with pink squirrels. "Tell me this."

"Yeah?"

"Why did those girls follow you like you were someone?"

"Aren't we all someone?"

She playfully scowled. "I just—"

"Just what?" I prompted, realizing she really didn't have the faintest clue that I sang, that all my songs ran up and down the billboards like a hamster on a wheel.

It was refreshing. For the first time in a long time, I was looking at a woman who might see me as Jacob first.

For so long, I've tried to keep most of me private so no one could destroy who I was. It didn't matter if they trashed the image I'd put out there because that wasn't who I was. But Lana made me want to share the real me, and I'd only just met her.

"Well, this *someone* is going to get up on stage and

make a fool of herself."

I smiled, knowing Lana couldn't make a fool of herself even if she tried.

"Good Luck. Break a leg and all that."

She took a deep breath and walked toward the stage.

Lana quickly climbed the steps, and immediately, the bar quieted. All you had to do was look at Lana, and she took your breath away.

But I was dying to know what song she'd chosen.

And then it happened.

Her fingers wrapped around the microphone. She took a breath and scanned the audience as the familiar beat of Nancy Sinatra's *These Boots are Made for Walking* rolled over the speakers. Her slender hips started shaking to the rhythm, and the crowd went wild.

My knee bobbed to the tempo of the familiar song as her voice filled the bar.

It was like the heavens opened up. Her hips swayed, her legs skated from one side to the next as she sang her heart out.

Joy.

It was pure joy that washed through me as I watched Lana start stomping as the final bit of the song carried out.

The bar erupted into craziness, and I knew if she had just one little shot at singing, truly singing, there could be something there for her.

Our eyes connected, and my pulse quickened as I watched her hand the microphone to the next singer.

Lana nearly skipped to the table and landed in the chair with a happy thud. Her beautiful voice still swirled in my mind as I watched her catch her breath.

I leaned forward. "Tell me this."

She eyed me. "What's that?"

"Was that song a warning?"

CHAPTER FIVE

Lana

My head throbbed, and I vaguely remembered doing my best to flirt with a cowboy last night.

A very sexy cowboy.

I also remembered that he was a complete gentleman as I embarrassed myself on stage.

But I couldn't help myself. It was like I'd kept that part of me bottled up at the inn for all these years. The truth was that I loved to sing, but I only did it when I was absolutely, positively certain that no one could hear me.

It took the drinks to get me to that next level. This

wasn't the first time this combination had proven deadly. I wasn't a drinker, didn't really care for the taste, but if there was a karaoke machine around, I suddenly became a fan favorite of whatever drink special the place had.

I let out a groan and pushed my temples with my fingertips. I had about ten minutes to pull myself together to pay my respects to Lars and his family. The memorial was more of a friendly gathering hosted out by the lake here on the property.

I still didn't quite understand this sudden pull I'd had to say goodbye to Lars, but in my heart, he was my first. I just didn't quite expect him to be my last.

Okay, it wasn't quite that bad, but I rarely had time or energy to go out on dates with everything I had to do at the inn. The load had been lightened since Samantha came on board, but I still managed the same excuses for why I didn't want to meet a guy, which told me I really wasn't that interested.

Jacob flashed into my head, and a smile touched my lips. Everything about him screamed experience, and I was pretty sure I wouldn't be able to handle him.

Although, that wasn't what I was thinking last night when I agreed to go out with him tonight after the memorial service.

Which in itself was odd. I'm going on a date with a near-stranger after saying goodbye to a man who'd shaped most of my dating career, which was to say, I didn't have one.

I pulled a black sweater out of my suitcase and put it on over my black pants and blouse before heading out the door of my hotel room. As I made my way toward the exit for the hotel, my stomach tightened. What was I even going to say to Lars's friends and family? What if he had a wife and kids? The thought terrified me. Maybe this was a really bad idea.

By the time I'd pushed myself outside, my hands were clammy, and my stomach sloshed with a mixture of apprehension and fear.

No. I drove all the way to Montana to pay my respects. I could do this.

I spotted a small gathering of people by the lake, along with several enlarged photos on easels. There were some beautiful flowers placed on tables near the photos, but there weren't any chairs. A bar from the hotel had been erected where people were getting refreshments.

I noticed the bartender from last night, but he wasn't behind the bar. He was standing by one of the photographs with a drink in his hand. He caught my gaze and smiled, motioning me over.

Relief spread through me when I realized I wasn't going to be alone quite like I thought.

I gave a quick wave and made my way over.

"How are you feeling?" he asked. "I told my girlfriend what I'd done, and she threw a pillow at me."

I grimaced and rubbed my temple. "Not that great. Thanks to you."

He laughed. "It got you up on the stage, didn't it?"

I smiled. "It did, and I'm kind of grateful for that. The best part is that those pink chipmunks—"

"Squirrels," he corrected.

I waved my hand. "Whatever. At least they made it so that I don't remember much of my disastrous rendition of Nancy Sinatra."

He smiled and shook his head. "You had the crowd going, and for the record, you have a beautiful voice."

"Ah, shucks." I drew a breath and glanced around the growing crowd.

"My name's Grey, by the way." He smiled.

"That's a nice name."

"It works for me. It's easy to remember." He took a sip of his drink, and I chuckled.

"Is his family here?" I whispered, scanning the people, talking, laughing, reminiscing.

Grey's eyes focused on me. "He doesn't really have any family. He was..." Grey bit his lip as he thought about what to say, knowing he had the same complex I did. "He was kind of a drifter."

I nodded, wondering what all that meant.

"See all these people?"

The crowd had really grown.

"My guess is ninety-nine percent of these people are his drinking buddies." He shook his head. "There for you when the times are good and fun, but they tend to disappear if any sort of depth is involved."

I shook my head slowly. "That's sad."

"Brings a good crowd to the memorial service, though."

"That's kind of a morbid thought. They're probably just relieved it's not them."

Grey nodded. "Lars led the happiest sad life you've ever seen. He was the first guy to make a big deal about stepping into the bar, and he was often the guy we had to lead out of the bar and call a ride home for." He looked around. "I shouldn't be saying this at the poor guy's funeral."

I touched his hand. "It's okay. It's just so... sad."

"I'm not sure he saw it that way. The guy lived in the moment. That's for sure."

I lowered my voice. "You know, I wasn't even sure he'd actually passed away. I actually wondered if he'd just faked his own death, you know?"

Grey nodded. "I know you weren't alone in that thinking."

"Did he have a wife or children?" I asked.

Grey's eyes widened. "Commitment was a four-letter word for the guy. I mean, if he had children, he certainly didn't know about it."

A couple stood next to us. The woman laughed and shook her head. "Well, dear, I don't think you'll be getting your five grand back."

My eyes darted over to the couple as the guy shrugged. "Does it really matter?"

"You tell me. It was your bright idea to give it to him."

A cold chill ran through me as I tore my gaze away and looked at Grey.

His eyes widened. "That's awkward."

A man wearing a leather vest clanked a glass with a pocketknife to get everyone's attention.

"I know we're all here to pay our final respects to Lars Stockton, which means I don't need to tell you that he was a wild and crazy guy. He was filled to the brim with an adventurous and carefree spirit. The man had his faults—we all do—but I know he'd want us to remember him as crazy Lars. He went out of this world like he came into it—buck naked."

The crowd chuckled, and I glanced around,

realizing there wasn't a tear to be shed. Would anyone actually miss Lars? Even though we always told everyone that my mom's memorial was purely a celebration of life service, tears flowed freely. The man giving the eulogy for Lars was rambling from one drinking story to the next, and my chest tightened as a deep hollowness filled me.

As I looked at the people standing around, I noticed some were glancing at their phones, chatting with whoever was next to them, or daydreaming toward the sky.

Tears slowly filled my eyes at the thought of how sad that would be. Where were his parents? I knew he had siblings too.

An overwhelming flood of emotions rushed through me as I thought about Lars and the loneliness he must have experienced through his years. Or maybe he didn't feel it because he drank so much. Maybe that was why he drank. He needed to numb whatever demons were deep inside.

I used the sleeve of my sweater for dabbing away the tears, and Grey looped his arm around my shoulder as the man with the vest continued his little anecdotes about the naked motorcyclist.

I sniffed and turned my head to Grey as he let loose of my shoulders.

"Was he serious? Lars was naked when they finally found him?" I whispered.

Grey nodded. "He was riding his bike in the buff, yeah. He was kind of known for that, but he eventually got the message from the police enough times that he limited riding naked to the dark."

The visual was more than I could bear. Nothing about that sounded appealing or sanitary.

"Wow. It's too bad my sister can't hear this stuff."

"Why's that?"

"She's a writer. She lives for this kind of thing." I shrugged.

I glanced at the crowd, who didn't even appear to be listening to the man talking, and my chest tightened even more at the thought of my own funeral.

Would there be tears or crocodile tears or no tears at all?

I drew a breath and shook my head as my heart ached at the thought of Lars living life, making it through life, as best he could. More tears ran down my cheeks as I thought about the rebel teenager that so many girls fawned over and how none of them were here.

I pushed a swallow down as I dabbed more tears away. I didn't even really know the man, but I'd missed him.

I wished I'd been there more for him. Or maybe that was exactly what he didn't want.

Another breath caught in my throat as the eulogy came to a crashing end of yet another drinking story. I suddenly felt very alone in the world.

The happy exterior I'd always done such a great job exuding didn't feel quite so legitimate as my eyes went from one enlarged photograph to the next of Lars. Everything just felt so final.

I started wondering if maybe the plastic smiles that often edged their way onto my features were the same type of coping mechanism, the same technique where I could push people away just enough. Maybe

Lars used alcohol, and I used my ability to smile no matter how much I wanted to scream.

Nervously glancing at Grey, I ran my hands down my black pants as I thought about what all this meant. Was I as happy as I thought I was, or was I living the happiest sad life I could muster?

The crowd went back to chatting among themselves, and from the sounds of it, most conversations weren't about Lars.

A sniffle came from out of nowhere when I thought about Lars, and I shook my head. "I can't believe I'm crying so much."

But why aren't more people sad about his death?

Grey smiled and nodded, glancing around the crowd. "It's nice to see some humanity. It feels like these people are just waiting for the sign that they can leave."

"I'm glad you think so." I saw a shadow of a figure in the distance walking around the lake, and I let out a sigh. "I feel silly for crying. This is a beautiful place. I just didn't expect his passing to hit me like this."

"It's natural. You probably knew him better than

most of these people." He drew a breath and shook his head. "The lake is beautiful. Think you'll want to stay when your trip's all over with?"

I laughed and shook my head. "I'm a creature of habit, and I'm pretty sure I'd start longing for my inn back home."

"An inn?" he asked.

"Yup. I run a little place called Cloudberry Inn with my sisters." Just mentioning the inn soothed me. I felt the tears begin to recede until I wondered if Lars ever had that comfort.

Grey's eyes filled with exuberance. "Wow. That's awesome. I've always thought that would be cool to do. My girlfriend and I dream about having a B&B or something."

"I say go for it." I nodded, feeling the wind dry my cheeks from the tears. "We inherited the inn from my parents. It's all I've ever known, so I'm assuming I love what I do."

Grey laughed as I caught sight of the man making his way along the lake.

It was Jacob.

Grey followed my gaze. "Oh, boy."

I chuckled and looked at Grey. "Yeah? Is he as much trouble as I think?"

"Honestly, Jacob's a good guy. Kind of new to town, even though he's owned a place here for ages." He narrowed his eyes on me. "You do know who he is, right?"

My brows shot up. "Should I?"

"Most women do."

I groaned. "So, he's Lars reincarnated."

Grey shook his head quickly. "Not even close. I don't know him very well, but I don't think he had time to really be here until recently," Grey revealed.

It made sense that some Silicon Valley guy wouldn't have time to actually enjoy his second home. Since Grey thought I should know who Jacob was, I made a mental note to look up CEOs of tech giants when I had a free second. I assumed that was why he lived in San Francisco, at least.

But why the cowboy hat?

"Well, I told him I'd go out with him tonight, but that was several squirrels committing on my behalf last night."

Grey smiled and nodded. "I think you should go for it. Plus, I'm not sure his ego could handle the rejection. He seemed to be mesmerized by you."

I rolled my eyes, which only made my headache worse. "Ha."

Jacob wandered through the people and gave a quick wave to us as he removed his cowboy hat.

His eyes locked on mine. "You've been crying."

I scowled. "Aren't you crashing a dead guy's party?"

Jacob smiled and nodded. "I suppose I am." He looked around. "But it looks like it's kind of breaking up."

Grey nodded. "I think it's disbanding pretty quickly, but I have a feeling they're all heading to the bar inside."

"Will you two be heading inside?" Jacob asked.

Grey shook his head. "I've gotta pick up some groceries on the way home, or my girlfriend will have my head. She invited my parents over last-minute and suddenly wants to impress them with some fancy dinner she's never made before."

I chuckled. "That ought to turn out well."

Grey nodded. "Hasn't yet."

Jacob laughed and nodded, turning to me. "What about you?"

"I don't think so. All the crying has exhausted me, and with what went down last night, I feel like the funeral could easily have been mine."

Grey and Jacob laughed.

"I'm sure I'll see you around while you're staying here." Grey gave a quick wave. "It was nice seeing you again."

I nodded. "Just sorry it was for a funeral."

Grey nodded. "Glad it wasn't mine. See? I did it again. Foot-in-mouth disease."

I chuckled, knowing it could have been me saying that just as easily.

"He's a nice guy," Jacob said, bringing his gaze back to mine as Grey trudged through the grass toward the parking lot.

"He really is, minus giving me so many drinks last night." I folded my arms over my chest. "I think I inadvertently challenged him last night when I told him I'd get up on stage if I'd had enough to drink."

"Mission accomplished." Jacob's eyes stayed on mine, and my chest started to loosen just a little. "I haven't been able to get your voice out of my head."

I laughed and glanced toward the lake. "I'm so sorry. It's probably like hearing a bunch of cats stuck in a pantry or something."

He touched my arm softly. "Not at all. Actually, I was kind of wondering what it would take to get you up on stage again."

"Not even for a million bucks," I assured him. "What it takes is liquid courage, and I feel so awful from last night's run-in with the cute rodent drink that I will never sing karaoke again."

"Never say never." A twinkle in his eyes made me wonder why he was so confident with that hunch of his.

I pulled my sweater closed as a breeze rolled over the small berm next to us.

"I'm pretty sure it's officially never. And why did I pick that song?" I groaned in exasperation. "I mean,

I love it, but it's not how I was feeling or anything."

"Maybe it was subconscious," he offered.

"Like how?" I shivered. "I swear I didn't have any feelings for him."

"Maybe not current feelings, but I could see how you might have felt like you needed to put Lars in his place. You know, I wouldn't have been thrilled if that had happened to me."

Jacob's blue eyes settled on mine, and I nodded.

"Or maybe you were sending me an indirect message." Jacob wiggled his brows.

"Are you always this observant?" I hugged myself and looked over his shoulder at the lake that was as still as glass despite the wind picking up.

"I have my days." He grinned, and I thought it was the cutest sight ever as he slipped his cowboy hat back on. "So, was the message directed at me?"

I laughed. "I'm not that clever." My brows arched, and I sucked in a breath. "Tell me this."

"Anything."

"If you lived in San Francisco all the time, why do you wear a cowboy hat?"

Jacob laughed and nodded. "Good question."

I looked around the empty area. "Was it just to fit in here? Because there really aren't that many men wearing them."

He laughed harder and nodded. "Something like that."

I studied him closely, noticing a story behind his eyes that I wanted to hear. I could see it unfolding with every blink. "So, why?"

"It's more of a profession thing, I guess."

I chuckled. "The techies like to dress up as rodeo stars?"

His brows lifted. "Techies?"

I squeezed myself a little more. "You're from San Francisco, so I just assumed you owned some tech company."

"You know what they say about assuming, right?"

I laughed and shook my head. "No, I haven't heard that one. So, are you a rancher, farmer, or rodeo legend?"

"None of the above."

"Hmm." I squinted at the sky while I tried to think

about what else might make a man need a cowboy hat. "You like to hide from people?"

"Sometimes," he revealed.

"Interesting." I wandered over to a row of photos of Lars as one toppled over.

I looked around, realizing no one had bothered to take them down, and it didn't look like anyone had any plans to do so. I bent down and picked up the one on the lawn before it blew into the lake.

Jacob came over and began removing them with me.

"It's so sad," I said, letting out a sigh. "I don't know the man Lars grew up to be, but I have never felt so alone and disconnected at a memorial service as I did today."

A chill ran over me.

Jacob collected the last couple of photos and took the ones I'd collected.

"Thankfully, it's not like I've been to a lot of funerals, but love tended to be the running theme." I shook my head.

"What did you feel here?" he asked, his voice

lowering.

"This is gonna sound awful." I shook my head. "But it almost felt like these people were relieved."

"Wow." Jacob ran his fingers along his chin. "That's really a brutal observation."

"And I feel awful for even voicing it." I drew a slow breath. "I just... I just think I had some fantasy about coming to this memorial service and seeing that Lars had grown up, that he'd stopped being..."

Jacob nodded. "Lars."

"Yup, and it doesn't sound like he ever did, and the friends he had were more surface-level than anything." I shook my head. "I don't know. Maybe I'm scared that I'm looking in a mirror."

Jacob's eyes fell to the photos he was holding.

"I don't see any resemblance. No goatee, mustache, or even a leather vest."

I chuckled and nodded. "Thank you. I waxed it off before my big vacation."

Jacob shook his head and smiled. "You're so different from any woman I've ever met."

My brows pulled together, and I tilted my head.

"You must not get around much. I'm pretty average."

Jacob shifted the large photos as the wind picked up. "What if we start our date early?"

CHAPTER SIX

Jacob

I couldn't get Lana out of my head all night. I'd barely slept a wink.

I'd walked out the back door of my place in hopes that I'd run into Lana early when I saw a bunch of people congregating along the lake by the lodge.

And I did, and here I was staring at her, hoping that I didn't look as desperate as I felt.

I had no idea what had gotten into me, but I had to see her again. Maybe to see if what kept me up all night was true.

Lana smiled and nodded. "I'd like that very

much."

"Really?" I couldn't hide my surprise.

She shrugged. "Yeah. Why not? I don't have the faintest idea where to go or what to do around here."

"Nice." I juggled all the enlarged photos I'd taken from her. "I'll just go inside with these."

Lana looked down at her clothes. "Do you mind if I go change? I'm not an all-black kind of girl, and this feels like I've just been to a funeral."

I laughed. "Not to mention that you *have* just been to a funeral."

She grinned. "Exactly." Her eyes fell to the stack of photos. "Thanks for taking that inside for me. I just thought it was kind of weird to leave them outside where they could blow away or whatever."

Lana's kindness made me stop and think for a second. She hadn't seen the man who'd treated her terribly in high school since high school, and yet, she showed more respect for him than any of his supposed friends.

"Totally. I'll just meet you in the lobby."

She nodded, opening the door for us. "It might

take me a few minutes. I'm not the best at packing, so finding socks that match or even shoes can be a challenge."

I smiled and watched her walk toward a corridor while I wandered over to the front desk.

"Hey there, Mr. Miller." A man smiled at me from behind the counter.

Considering I didn't have a room here, I suppose I wasn't as unrecognizable as I thought in Montana.

I smiled and placed the stack of Lars on the counter. "The group having the memorial service just left these out there, and my friend was worried they'd blow away."

The man looked at the photos and shook his head. "Such a shame."

"You knew him?" I asked.

"He was somewhat of a legend around here." He looked like he wanted to elaborate, but he kept his lips tight.

"I've heard that." I nodded and glanced behind me. "Well, thanks again for taking care of these."

He nodded. "Absolutely, sir. Umm..."

"Yeah?"

"Do you mind if I get an autograph? My sister had your picture on her wall growing up."

I'd heard that so many times, and it still made me laugh. "Sure."

He slid me a piece of paper, and I scribbled out the woman's name and signed mine.

"Thanks so much, Mr. Miller. This gets me off the hook for her birthday."

"Awesome." I nodded and wandered over to the seating in the lobby.

A few people did a double-take in my direction, but I wanted to believe it was because they liked the furniture near the fireplace.

Even after all these years, I hadn't become used to being recognized or photographed. It was probably why I'd spent so much time on the bus most of my adult life.

But I was sick of it. I was sick of everything. The smell of the diesel from the bus. The smell of the bus. The tight quarters. Not knowing the city I was in until my manager told me.

After about ten minutes, I leaned back and kicked my legs out as I pulled my hat over my brows.

I thought back to my parents and how happy they'd always been. It didn't matter if they had ten cents in the bank account or ten million. All they cared about was being in love, being there for one another. The happiest moment of my life was paying off their home. I'd offered to buy them a larger one, but they refused to leave the one they'd raised my sister and me in.

And I understood it.

But I wasn't sure I could do the same.

Ever since I'd lost my sister, it was hard to go back there, to go back to the place where all the memories we'd had lived on. I couldn't walk down the hall or enter the kitchen without seeing the ghost of Evie. My sister's name was Evelyn, but she'd always been Evie to me.

My chest tugged at the thought, and I cleared my throat and sat up just as Lana's voice brought me back to earth.

"Hey there, city boy turned country." She laughed,

sitting next to me as I pushed my hat back.

I grinned. "If you only knew."

"Why don't you enlighten me?"

"It's more fun to keep you guessing."

Lana's eyes danced at the thought, and she smiled wider. "If I don't guess by the end of my vacation, you're going to have to tell me. Deal?" She held out her pinky.

I glanced at mine and looped it around hers.

The last time I'd done that was with Evie. She was eleven. I was sixteen. I pushed away the thought and nodded.

"Deal."

"What do you have planned for us, Jacob?"

Her big doe eyes looked into mine. She'd scooped her hair into a ponytail and was wearing a pair of cropped jeans and a cotton plaid shirt that she'd unbuttoned just enough. I'd like to think I captured it all without ever taking my eyes off hers.

"It's kind of up to you. I have some kayaks and a canoe up the way."

Her brows shot up. "At your house?"

I nodded. "Too soon?"

She laughed. "A tiny bit. I want to make sure I won't turn up missing."

"And how many dates does that take before you're sure of something like that?"

Lana looked toward the ceiling and puckered her mouth as she pretended to count. "Well, if I were to be completely honest, I haven't been on enough dates in a row to know."

"Ah, so you're the picky type."

She pretended to scowl. "Not picky. Too busy having a life separate from a man to care."

I chuckled. "Of course. The old I-don't-need-a-man trick."

"Okay, that sounded awful the way it came out." She grinned. "But nobody *needs* a man."

Seeing her feistiness light up made me really happy that I convinced her to come on our date early.

"Of course not." I grinned. "But we men can make things kind of fun."

She smiled at me and held my gaze. "Tell me more about this fun."

"How about I show you?"

Lana's eyes narrowed on me. "Music to my ears."

I stood and held my hand out to help her out of the leather chair, noticing her eyelids still had a touch of pink from crying earlier.

Her narrow fingers wrapped around mine, and the sweet smell of honeysuckle wafted from her ponytail.

"There's a place down the road that rents canoes and kayaks, if that sounds good. Then you won't be confronted with the terrible decision of coming back to my place." I watched her reaction. "Or we could do horseback riding the other way up the road."

Her eyes lit up. "Both sound good."

"Does this mean I might get a two-date commitment out of you?"

"Maybe." She smirked. "But I have rules, you know."

"Rules?"

"You heard me."

I laughed and took a step back as I removed my hat. "Let me have 'em."

"You heard the first one."

"Don't go back to a strange man's house."

She nodded.

I laughed. "It's actually a really good one."

"The second rule is to not let the man pay for dinner on the first date."

"Because you don't want to feel like you owe me anything."

She grinned wider. "These rules actually came from my mom like fifteen years ago."

"What? When you were like six?"

Lana smiled. "What? Now you're saying I look really young instead of old? It wasn't long ago that you called me Ma'am."

"In all fairness, you look perfect. I'm not good with ages." But now that she brought it up, I did wonder, not that it mattered. "And Ma'am was just how I was raised. My dad would kick me in the butt if I didn't call any and every female Ma'am, and that was only if I didn't know their last name to call them Mrs. or Miss."

"He sounds sweet."

I nodded, not wanting to reveal too much about my family. "He is. Okay, next rule."

"There's too many to list. Let's see, don't kiss until date four. Don't say yes if you don't actually like the man." She laughed.

"Doesn't sound unreasonable."

"I have a confession," she whispered.

"Lay it on me."

"I haven't had to use those rules for years. I need this vacation badly. I've been so busy making everyone else's vacations amazing that I forgot about taking one of my own."

I wasn't sure if this was a good time to bring up a funeral joke.

I glanced at the stack of Lars's photos still at the front counter and thought better of it.

"Can you hold hands on a first date?"

She grinned. "Technically, it's our second."

I slipped my hand over hers and laughed. "I like the way you think."

"Well, I've only got two weeks to kick up my heels."

I laughed and shook my head as I led her out of the lobby. "I hope I can help."

She eyed me as we made our way into the parking lot. "Something tells me you will be able to do just fine in that department."

"Good." I led her to my pickup, and she whistled.

"Boy, you're really carrying this cowboy theme to the end and back."

I laughed and shook my head. "You'd be surprised at how handy they are in Montana."

"We'll see about that. I think you're just living your best life as a wannabe cowboy." She climbed into the passenger seat as I walked around to the driver's seat.

When I slid in, she was texting on her phone. Her eyes caught mine, and she smiled. "I'm letting my sisters know your license plate number to go along with your full name."

I laughed and shook my head until I realized she probably wasn't kidding. "Oh, you're serious."

She giggled. "You'll never know."

"Somehow, I believe you."

I put the truck in reverse and followed the signs toward the ranch I'd seen several times. I'd never been, but I hoped they had openings.

"Do you do a lot of riding?" she asked.

"When I was a kid, I worked at some stables so I could ride for free."

The answer seemed to surprise her.

"Really?" She turned in the seat and kept her eyes on me.

I nodded. "Yeah. Our family had an abundance of love and a little bit less in the penny department. I had a favorite. His name was Raven. He was a stallion."

She chuckled. "Of course he was."

I caught her gaze and laughed. "I swear from the moment we've met, you've made me feel a lot lighter."

"Well, that hat does look heavy."

I smiled. "What about you?"

"Kind of the same thing. Most of our money was always tied up with the inn, but we basically lived in the middle of farm country, so I managed to get my horse fix." She eyed me. "I bet you made a cute little boy, always dressing up like a cowboy."

I laughed. "What if I told you I was a super famous country singer?"

She chuckled, throwing her head back as they turned into a fit of giggles.

"Well, then I'd tell you that I'm glad I gave my sister your information."

Her answer made me laugh. "Yeah? Why's that?"

"You might not be all there." She tapped her temple, and I laughed.

"Yeah, well, I just crashed a dead guy's party, so you might be onto something."

Lana's cheeks reddened. "And here I thought you happened to randomly walk along the lake."

"Then that's what happened." I glanced at her before turning down the long dirt road toward the stables.

"This is a great way to turn my vacation around." She sighed a happy sigh, and I nodded.

"Your vacation can probably only get better from this morning."

She turned to me and nodded. "Good point."

"It's kind of a good way to go through life," I

offered.

She laughed and looked out her window toward the stables. "Yeah? Keep your bar set super low so that anything will seem like an improvement?"

"Something like that."

I pulled in front of a log cabin where the office was, and Lana hopped out. I walked around to meet her, and she looked at my boots.

"At least you're dressed for the occasion." She slid her hands into her pockets and rocked back on her sneakers as someone caught her eye. "Look, it's your twin."

I glanced over to the office where an older woman with a pink Western shirt, Wrangler jeans, and cowgirl boots made her way over. She removed her cowgirl hat and waved as I kept in a snicker.

Lana eyed me. "Told ya."

The woman smiled and looked me up and down. "Aren't you dressed for the occasion?"

Lana giggled.

"You here for a ride?" the woman asked.

"I didn't make any reservations, but I saw your

sign."

"You're in luck. We have two horses available." She smiled with a twinkle in her eye, and I realized she'd just recognized me. My stomach tightened at the thought of her saying something to let Lana in on my secret.

"What's your experience level?" she asked.

"It sounds like we were both experts at the age of eleven," Lana said, laughing.

"Ah, good. The two pintos I have will be perfect for you."

"I love pintos," Lana gushed.

"Carl and Jaqueline are sweethearts," the woman confirmed.

Lana lit up, and I knew this date would be a winner.

CHAPTER SEVEN

Lana

For a man who spent most of his life in San Francisco, he certainly seemed agile and highly skilled at directing his horse. I hadn't been on a horse since I was a teenager, and it wasn't quite like riding a bike. Thankfully, Jaqueline wasn't a quick trotter. She enjoyed stopping in the middle of the trail and just staring off into the distance.

I very much related to her. It was a pastime I'd quite enjoyed at Cloudberry Inn.

Jacob's horse came to a stop in front of me, and Jacob looked over his shoulder.

"Seriously? She stopped again?" His brows arched.

I leaned forward and scratched her neck. "She's tired. I'm not light."

"Well, if you think you're not light, then my horse hates me right about now."

I chuckled. "No. I know I'm as wiry as they come, but I wouldn't enjoy hauling anyone around no matter their weight."

Jacob smiled wider, and all kinds of butterflies bumped into each other in my belly. I don't think I'd had a reaction like that purely from a glance.

"How about here for a picnic?" Jacob asked, pointing at the meadow right off the trail.

Sparse wildflowers scattered among the tangled, dried grass. It was beautiful, but I'd be lying if I didn't at least voice my concern.

"Are there rattlesnakes out there?"

Jacob slid off his horse and tied him to a spindly-looking ponderosa pine.

I giggled, getting off Jacqueline. "Do you really think Carl couldn't just bolt and take that tree with him? Even Jaqueline could give the sapling a run for her money."

Jacob eyed my horse. "I'll take my chances, and it's not a sapling. It's more like a teenager. And you never know. There could be."

Jacob tied Jaqueline next to Carl and grabbed a bag of sandwiches and snacks they had available for purchase back at the office.

I eyed him. "Could be what?"

"Could be rattlesnakes out there. You asked if there could be rattlesnakes."

I laughed. "Right, and that was *not* the answer to give me."

"Do I truly think we'll run into one? No. They generally like to snuggle up to boulders, but it always pays to keep an ear out. They are the prairie rattlers, so they hang out in tall grass and sun, but my bet is there over by that pile of rocks."

"Says the city boy who bumps into red trolleys more often than poisonous snakes."

He smiled, and it made me feel all kinds of happiness. "Just don't use a rock as a picnic table, and we should be fine."

I glanced at Jaqueline. "Maybe I'll eat on my horse."

Jacob laughed and nodded. "We could."

"Really? You wouldn't think I'm a weenie?"

"I didn't say that." Jacob smirked, and every fiber of my being felt like it was being pulled to him like some giant forcefield where he was the center of my world.

Was this what happened on vacations? People just threw caution to the wind and wanted to jump any good-looking male who came their way?

I eyed Jacob and wondered if he were Big Fork's tourist trap.

"Why are you looking at me like that?" Jacob unwrapped a couple of sandwiches and pulled out a bag of chips and a bag of carrots.

The blood rushed to my cheeks, and I dropped my gaze to the dirt, focusing on a particularly dull pebble.

He handed me the food, and I balanced all the baggies so I could get to the carrots. I immediately started gnawing on them as Jaqueline turned and neighed in my direction.

Jacob started laughing and shook his head as I climbed back on my horse and took another bite of carrot.

"What's so funny?" I asked, smiling at Jacob.

"Those were for the horses." He eyed the orange sticks in my hand.

I glanced down at the unpeeled carrot and groaned. "I wondered why it wasn't peeled."

Jacob's laughter came from deep in the belly, and all I could do was wipe the tears off my cheek from nonstop laughter.

These were the tears I needed today.

A snort escaped my lips, which only made Jacob laugh harder as I slid off Jaqueline and apologized to her as I fed her the remaining carrots I had. I left my sandwich bag and chips on the saddle while Jacob fed his horse.

"Have you composed yourself yet?" I teased Jacob, feeding Jaqueline.

"I don't know if I ever will." Jacob's eyes

connected with mine. "You just make me smile."

I shrugged and smiled. "Could be worse."

"If date two is this fun with you, I can't wait for date three."

My brows shot up in surprise. "Date three?"

"Well, you said you wanted to go on the lake too..." His voice trailed off as Carl finished off the last of Jacob's carrots. "I assumed it would be with me."

I chuckled, remembering what he'd said to me last night. "Well, you know what they say about assuming."

He laughed as the familiar joke was thrown back at him. "Nice."

My horse polished off her last carrot from my palm. I nearly pranced to the saddle, grabbed my sandwich and chips, and walked over to Jacob.

"I'm ready." I glanced toward the pasture. "Let's go eat some sandwiches among the wildflowers and live on the wild side."

Jacob grimaced. "Honestly, once you mentioned the snakes, I..." He shook his head.

My eyes widened. "Really?"

"Nah. Just kidding." He shrugged and smiled, grabbing a blanket that had been provided. "You know, if you want, I could give you a piggyback ride. Then it's just me and my cowboy boots in danger."

"It seems like my city slicker is a lot more prepared than I am." I smiled as he studied me. "But I will take you up on the offer."

He put the rolled-up blanket under his arm as I jumped around him and secured my legs in front of him.

"Here's the thing, though. If we have to take these kinds of precautions just to have lunch, should we be doing it?" I asked, worrying that a prairie rattler was about to strike at Jacob any moment.

Jacob held my knees as I gave his waist the death grip while holding two sandwiches and two bags of chips.

"Just don't trip," I reminded him.

"Any other rules?" he teased as he walked us off the trail.

"Well, maybe a place in the shade. Snakes don't like to be cold, right?"

Jacob laughed and shook his head. "Had I known it would be this easy to have you wrap your legs around me, I would have warned you back at the lodge."

I chuckled, enjoying the moment. I'd never been one to be forward or overly flirty, but there was something with Jacob that felt so comfortable while also feeling like I was on the verge of falling off a cliff.

"How about this area?" He found a somewhat shady area that had mostly dirt and gravel with a few sparse blades of grass.

"Perfect. There's nowhere for anything to hide."

"I thought you might like that."

I reluctantly slid from Jacob's waist and tried to pretend the mere act of being entangled around him didn't make me all kinds of crazy. Heat pooled in my belly, and I tried to distract myself with the ham sandwich he handed me before spreading out the plaid blanket.

"Well, it's been a really interesting day so far." Jacob helped me sit before kneeling with one leg up. He looked over the prairie by peering under the brim of his cowboy hat.

I couldn't help but laugh. "You know, if you ever wanted to model for album covers, I really think you have the lone cowboy look all figured out."

Jacob turned his attention to me and smiled. "Yeah? Why's that?"

"You have this whole sultry, mysterious stare down. Plus, you look good in rodeo wear."

He laughed and took a bite of his sandwich.

"Even that was manly." I nodded toward the sandwich, and he laughed harder.

"How can eating a sandwich look manly?"

"For starters, you didn't nibble it. You clutched the bread fully in your hands and took charge, nearly ripping your bite off the rest of the sandwich."

Jacob grinned and shook his head. "I don't think I've ever had a woman analyze me this much."

"That's no fun."

He shook his head. "No, it's not."

I wondered just how many women had had the opportunity.

Not that it mattered.

I was in Montana on vacation, and I had no idea what he was here for, other than that he had a vacation home here that he suddenly wanted to be his permanent residence.

"So, when are you going to do the big reveal to me?" I asked, taking a bite of the sandwich.

"What big reveal?" he asked.

"You know. What you do to allow you to have a vacation home in Montana."

His eyes caught mine as he finished his sandwich. "I already did."

I scowled, racking my brain. "No, you didn't."

He nodded. "Yeah, I did."

I took another bite of my sandwich, trying to think back to all of our conversations.

"So, you are a techie?"

He shook his head and opened the bag of chips. "Nope."

Then it hit me. The expression on his face when he was scanning the prairie, looking all sexy.

"I know what it is. You looked like a man on the lam, searching for a place you won't be found."

"Does that make you nervous?"

I smiled and shook my head. "Should it?"

"Probably not, but you're getting warmer."

I didn't necessarily want to pry. Whatever fun and flirtatious thing we had going wasn't going to go anywhere. He didn't have to tell me a thing.

But there was something behind his gaze that made me want to know so much more.

"It's not my place, but I'm nosy."

"What's that?" he asked, turning completely toward me. Somehow, it felt like the rest of the world just fell away, like this vast amount of land surrounding us shrank to a little island where only he and I existed.

"Why does it look like you're always trying to run away or hide?"

His lips parted, and he closed them quickly. "I didn't know it did."

My head cocked slightly. "Well, maybe not to most people, but it's just something I see."

I polished off my sandwich as I thought back to how he even darted away from the batch of teenagers the first time I spotted him.

"I guess my life has often put me in the center of everything, and I'm just to the point where I'm ready to have some time for myself."

"Except that you went out to the bar, so maybe you don't want to hide as much as you think," I pointed out.

He laughed and nodded. "What can I say? I'm complicated."

I believed him.

"Tell me about this inn of yours."

The moment he mentioned the inn, comfort and familiarity filled me to the brim.

"It's a beautiful place set in the middle of tulip fields. We've managed to grow the inn, add rooms, add gardens. It's become quite the destination." I smiled. "A lot of that has to do with my one sister coming back."

His brows peaked. "Coming back?"

I suddenly wished I'd kept my mouth shut, but that was the problem with me. Things just rolled out.

"She... well, it's complicated, or should I say I'm

complicated?"

Jacob laughed and plucked a white flower.

"My two sisters." I cleared my throat. "Well, three sisters." I eyed him. "I just found out I had an extra one out there."

Jacob's gaze snapped to mine. "How do you have an extra one?"

"I told you it was complicated. Too much for this trail ride." I twisted my lips into a sloppy smile as he handed me the white flower.

"You're on vacation. I don't mean to stress you out. You can tell me when you're ready or not. But just for fun, here's another clue about me."

I smiled and took the delicate flower from him.

"This is a clue?" I asked.

He nodded.

It's a flower, which is a plant. Weed is a flower. He lived in California. Weed is legal in California.

"Why are you staring at me like that?" he asked, laughing.

"Are you a drug grower?"

He cocked his head slightly and stared at the

flower. "What kind of flower do you think that is?"

I glanced at the flower and smiled. "I have no idea, but—"

Jacob laughed and shook his head. "No, I'm not a weed farmer."

"Is that the technical term?" I smiled.

He shrugged. "Beats me, but you have a really interesting mind."

I beamed as if that were the best compliment I'd ever received in my life.

In fact, I was pretty sure it was.

CHAPTER EIGHT

Jacob

I stared at the clock in my kitchen. It had done nothing but tick impossibly slowly these last four hours. After dropping off Lana yesterday back at the lodge, I came home and tried to sleep her off.

But I couldn't.

There was something absolutely, insanely devastating about her. Beyond the obvious fact that she was beautiful, funny, and smart, her mind was like a treasure trove of greatness. I never knew where our conversations were headed. I could never guess what the next thing out of her mouth would be.

My only hope was that none of that would change once she found out who I was. It shouldn't, but it always did.

Granted, I'd never just bumped into someone like this before. Everything in my life had always been created, manufactured, or fabricated for other people's benefit. New A-list actress? I've got a guy for you. Just beginning in the music business? I've got a guy for you. Need a distraction? I've got a guy for you.

The problem was that I was always the guy agents wanted to hook their clients up with, and I always fell for it.

Whether it was the hopeless romantic in me or the needy musician in me, I didn't know. All I knew was that if I had to have one more shallow conversation about lip gloss or what someone wore on a red carpet, I'd lose it.

The time had definitely come to step back from the only world I knew before I wanted to annihilate it, and I was only half kidding.

So back to waiting for the last six hours in a bout of nonstop caffeine drinking since I couldn't sleep past six o'clock this morning with nothing more than pure anticipation.

I was like a kid waking up on Christmas morning, but it was so I could see Lana again.

Just her name made me wonder what the day would be filled with.

This would be date number three in her mind. Would there be a date number four?

What if there wasn't?

The thought nearly did me in.

No. There had been chemistry between us. She wouldn't just leave me hanging. Would she? She might.

That was the thing about Lana Roberts. I had no idea what to expect from her.

The thought made me smile.

I glanced at the clock.

Screw it. I'm gonna head to the lodge early. I could always grab breakfast by myself if she doesn't want to head off to the lake early.

I walked over to the fridge and grabbed the snack baggies I'd filled up last night for our time on the lake.

I was sure to get carrots.

Just the memory of her eating the horse's carrots made me smile as I made my way into the family room. I picked up my shirt from the couch and pulled it over my head. I'd managed a shower at the crack of dawn this morning, but I couldn't be bothered with getting dressed all the way because I immediately started daydreaming about a woman I shouldn't be pursuing.

It wasn't like we had all the time in the world. In less than two weeks, she'd be headed back to Washington.

This little adventure was meant to go nowhere. It had all the framework to drive my hopes right into the ground, so I needed to make this a vacation she remembered since nothing much else would come from it.

Or could there be something more?

I rolled my eyes at myself and reached for the truck keys on the coffee table.

Did showing up early reek of desperation?

I smiled and shrugged, pushing my hat on.

This thing had become my security blanket. I'd used it to camouflage myself for so long that I wasn't even sure what I would do without it. It probably sounded crazy, but it was true.

And I kind of liked Lana's flipping me shit over it.

Just the thought touched a smile to my lips as I made my way to the garage.

This house was certainly a lot larger than my San Francisco pad, but it felt way homier. I wondered if Lana would actually allow herself to come over.

I smiled at the thought and climbed into my truck as I pushed the garage door opener and light spilled into the large space.

The sound of my engine roared to life, and I reversed out of my garage as I blasted on the radio.

The beat of the song rattled through me as I tapped the steering wheel and thought about the industry that had given me so much. I would always be grateful for the fans and the record companies that helped propel me forward and the radio stations that played my songs, but I was tired.

I was tired of being something I wasn't.

I wasn't a product.

I wasn't a machine.

As the music carried me toward the lodge, I pulled into the parking lot and found a spot near the entrance.

I sucked in a breath and hoped I wasn't about to make a fool of myself, or worse, creep her out.

But I wasn't a creepy dude, was I?

I shook my head and chuckled as I shut off the truck and jumped out.

I let out the air I'd sucked in and started toward the lobby when I heard a wave of squeals splinter through the air.

I spun quickly around to see the same group of girls from the other night.

"Shit," I muttered to myself, scanning the parking lot distance to the door.

There was nowhere to hide, nowhere to run, and they were coming fast.

There were only five or six, but they sounded like an army of a hundred, and their eager eyes looked like they'd eat me for lunch and spit me out.

This time, their phones were out in full view as they booked toward me, undoubtedly videoing me.

"Just get it over with, Jacob," I whispered to myself.

I didn't need a viral video of me running and hiding from a bunch of teenage girls.

The sooner I gave them what they wanted, the sooner they'd leave me alone.

"Jacob Miller," one of the shorter ones shrieked.

I stood as still as a statue and readied my position, praying they wouldn't jump on me.

That had happened more times than I'd care to remember.

I raised my hand up and tipped my hat. "Hey."

More shrieks erupted, and I glanced around the parking lot, hoping that Lana wasn't out for a morning jog or something.

"Are you really him?" another one asked, her voice shaking.

And that was when it hit me.

This was nothing but pure joy for these kids. There wasn't any motive. It was just a fun day in

Montana.

I smiled and nodded. "I'm really him."

"Would you sign this for me?" The girl shoved her phone at me.

"The phone?" I asked.

She scowled as if I were as dumb as a ton of bricks. "No, the case."

"Oh, right. Sorry. It's early. Do you have a pen?"

Another one pulled a marker out of her bag and handed it to me.

"My mom is going to be so jealous," she said, smiling.

"She loves old people's music."

I stopped mid-signing. "Old people music?"

"Oh, sorry. I didn't mean you were old."

"I'm only thirty-seven."

Another one giggled. "That's old."

"Yeah. You're like twenty-three years older than me." She laughed.

"Then why are you screaming?" I asked, genuinely curious.

"You're cute and famous."

"Ah," I said, handing back the phone cover.

"Me too?" She handed me an envelope from her purse to sign. "Can you make it out to my mom?"

I laughed to myself and shook my head. "Yeah, what's her name?"

I signed a few more things they'd managed to round up and wondered how this all just happened. I'd left San Francisco thinking I was the bomb and now stood in the middle of Montana doing some serious soul-searching.

Did the six-hour flight suddenly make me over the hill?

I grinned at the thought and walked into the lobby just as Lana started toward the café.

It was like suddenly, everything in the world turned right-side up. I kind of liked the idea of being more mature.

Would she see me that way?

"Hey, Lana."

She stopped and turned. The moment our eyes connected, a big smile covered her lips, and I was certain I was the luckiest man in the world.

"You're early," she said, glancing at her phone.

"I was hungry. I couldn't sleep." I looked around the lobby. "Mainly, I was hungry. Thought maybe you'd like to join me, but I see you're already headed there, so maybe I'll join you?"

Her smile only widened as my heart felt like it would beat out of my chest.

"I'd love that."

"Yeah?" Whether it was the encounter out in the parking lot or just Lana, I suddenly wondered where my cool card had gone.

"Totally, and you can tell me why you couldn't sleep."

I caught up with her and laughed. "I don't think you're ready for that."

"You'd be surprised. Remember? I have had my fair share of surprises, including a new sister?"

I laughed as we sat ourselves near the wall of windows that overlooked the lake. Several tables were filled with families and couples, and I wondered if I'd ever have that.

Lana caught my gaze, and a smile fell to her lips,

but she didn't say anything as she opened one of the menus the hostess just gave us.

"Mmm... I feel like a Belgian waffle with strawberries and extra whipped cream."

A woman after my own heart. Whipped cream? I was sure that stuff was illegal in Hollywood.

"Yeah? I'll one-up you."

"Try me." She narrowed her eyes on me.

"Eggs Benedict, side of sausage and hashbrowns."

"I'll take a side of bacon with mine." She flashed a devilish grin. "And I'll do two eggs, over hard, and I'll have one of your muffins."

"Wait. What?" I laughed. "How is that fair?"

"How's it not?" She laughed.

"Only if I get half of your waffle."

"Deal, as long as I get some of your sausages," she added.

"I don't think I'm coming out of this fair and square."

She took a deep breath as the waitress came over and served us coffee and took our orders. When the server left, she studied me for a few seconds.

"So, why couldn't you sleep?"

I smiled. "Lots of things on my mind."

Lana nodded and grinned. "Ah, the ever-present vague response."

I took a sip of coffee and set it down. "I thought I had things all figured out when I came here."

She nodded.

"Then I met you."

A spark of intrigue darted through her gaze.

"Is that good or bad?"

I laughed and shook my head. "I have no idea, but it's nice."

She nodded. "I thought I had things all figured out when I left the inn too, and then I got all sentimental at a funeral."

"Not too unusual," I pointed out.

Lana took a sip of coffee, and I couldn't help but notice her lush lips.

"Do you think I can get you back on the stage before you go?" I asked.

"For another rendition of Nancy Sinatra?" She laughed. "I don't think so."

"Come on. The crowd loved you. I loved you. Your voice is amazing."

And the truth was since I'd heard her sing, lyrics started flooding my mind nonstop. Not that I planned to do anything with them.

She rolled her eyes. "I can only imagine what I looked like up there belting out that song."

I cocked my head in awe. "Seriously? You were sexy as hell."

Her brows shot up. "Sexy?"

"Very."

"You might have had more drinks than I did."

"You're not very good at hearing nice things about yourself."

She shrugged. "I'd spent my entire childhood hearing how awesome my sister was and most my adult life wishing I could trade my life with her." Her eyes widened, and she quickly slipped her hands over her mouth. "Well, not really."

I shook my head. "It's okay. Your secret is safe with me."

She groaned and put her head in her hands. "It

didn't come out right."

"What does your sister do, exactly, that makes her life something you want?"

Lana toyed with her napkin for a few seconds, and I had this sudden need to comfort her, but I knew that would be ridiculous in the middle of a restaurant.

"It's not what she does or who she is, I suppose." Lana brought her gaze up to mine. "She's a writer, a really good writer, but I despise writing. I love to read, though."

I smiled. "Okay. You're right. I'm not following."

"See? I have that ability. I can confuse just about anyone given enough time."

"Well, I have a lot of time and an overabundance of patience."

"From the time my sister was a teenager, she's hit all the bestseller lists. She was like a wonder child who turned into a wonder adult."

"I think you're pretty wonderful."

"Thank you." Lana's lips curled into another beautiful smile. "I needed that."

"My pleasure."

"Anyway, she took all of my mom's time, which left my dad to run the inn, and in turn, left us to run the inn. I guess what I meant was that there are times in my life where I wish I had the freedom my sister has. She had a full life in New York, but when she decided she wanted a change, she just up and left, settled in at Cloudberry, and never looked back."

"And you've never been given that opportunity." I saw the wheels spinning behind Lana's eyes. She looked truly conflicted.

"I don't even think I want to leave Cloudberry, so I'm not sure what my hang-up is about." She shrugged. "But maybe it was just always the assumption that I'd be running it forever."

"Who's running it now?" I asked.

"My sister Samantha, the writer. She doesn't live on the premises, but we have someone there who does fill in since my other sister left and opened up a bookstore in the mountains far, far away."

"So, everyone has been able to fly the coop but you."

She straightened. "But I'm not sure I want to leave

the coop. I mean, what would I do? The inn is all I know."

"Nothing wrong with that."

When I looked at Lana, I felt such a deep connection. Once I'd made up my mind that I didn't want to tour anymore, I told myself I could spend all my days doing all the things I'd always wanted to do. The problem was that in the dead of night, as I lay in bed, I couldn't for the life of me figure out what that would be.

"I think we have a lot more in common than I realized."

"Yeah?" Lana asked, smiling. "Like what?"

"Neither of us knows what the heck we want out of life."

Lana laughed and picked up her coffee cup and raised it toward me. "Then a toast."

I raised my cup to meet hers, and the clink of the cups secured our bond. "To finding out what the heck it is that we think we're either missing or have right in front of us."

I smiled and nodded. "Cheers."

Her eyes stayed on mine before dropping to my lips for a brief second, and in even less time, I wondered if I'd imagined it all.

CHAPTER NINE

Lana

As I waddled out of the hotel behind Jacob, I had second thoughts about our next activity. I definitely wanted to go out on the lake, but I was pretty sure today wasn't the day to do it, but he looked so eager.

I didn't want to disappoint him, but I had to tell him.

"Hey, Jacob."

He spun around and smiled. His sunglasses hung on the collar of his shirt. "Yeah?"

"I hate to ask this, but we can have a raincheck on the lake?"

Immediate disappointment flooded his gaze.

I rubbed my stomach and grimaced. "I'm worried I'd sink the boat. I ate way too much." I glanced toward his truck. "But I saw on the map an awesome hiking trail. Maybe we could do that instead and the lake on a different date?"

Relief washed through his gaze, and I smiled.

"You're telling me I'm earning a fourth date before we've gone on our third?"

Somehow, Jacob had a way of making me feel like I was truly doing him a favor, like I was special, and I had no idea how he did it.

I scrunched my nose and nodded. "I guess that's what I'm saying."

"Tell me where you want to go, and I'll get us there."

"We could probably walk to the trailhead." I sucked in a breath. "But if we get pooped on our hike and have to walk back to the hotel, that wouldn't be fun."

"And then I might not get my fourth date."

I laughed as we made our way to his truck. I

hopped into the passenger seat and watched him hop into his seat.

He turned on the radio, and a guy's voice came over the radio belting out some sad song.

Jacob must have felt the same way about the music because his hand flew to the radio and turned it off.

"That guy's music always depresses me." I shook my head as I buckled. "I mean, don't get me wrong. He has a beautiful voice, whoever he is, but my word, his songs. It's like all the man has ever experienced in life is pain."

I glanced at Jacob, who smirked in my direction. "Yeah?"

"Don't you think? I mean, the songs are always sad."

He nodded, slipping his sunglasses over his eyes. "They do cover the nitty-gritty."

"That's a good way of putting it." I smiled and looked out the window before turning my gaze back to his. "I prefer to skip over the nitty-gritty and just enjoy life."

Jacob's gaze caught mine. I couldn't see his eyes behind the glasses, but I could feel it. "Or you just pretend to enjoy life."

It was like he'd read my soul and knew better than anyone, which was frightening. I'd only known him for a few days.

I snickered. "Well, just know that I don't listen to sad music. That's all I'm saying."

Jacob laughed. "So, you pretty much stay away from country."

"Pretty much." I grinned. "And like I said, the guy's voice is gorgeous, but dang. Just pop a couple of happy pills or something."

Jacob turned toward the gravel patch, where several cars had already parked. "Maybe the guy just hasn't met someone like you yet to turn his songs around."

Lana grinned. "I like that answer. Maybe you're right. What's the singer's name? I'll look him up."

Jacob parked and turned the truck off without answering, but he did grab a small cooler from behind us.

"I thought we'd have snacks on the lake, but we can eat them on the trail. I've got some granola bars, jerky, and your favorite, carrots."

I chuckled and blushed. "Aw, you remembered."

"Well, it was kind of hard to forget. You should have seen the look on poor Jaqueline's face."

I batted at him and shook my head. "I'm so full that I can't imagine I'll be able to even touch a carrot, but thank you for looking out for us."

Jacob smiled and climbed out of the truck. "Someone's gotta."

"Ouch." I laughed, hopping out of the truck. I quickly stuffed my phone into my back pocket before wandering over to Jacob's side. He shoved the food into a backpack.

"We have a lot of amazing hiking spots in Washington, even right near the inn."

"I bet." He nodded. "I've been there a few times. It's a beautiful place, but I've always just been stuck in the Seattle and Tacoma area."

"Really?" I smiled. "Well, if you're ever out that way, I'll have to show you the real parts of

Washington."

Jacob smiled. "It's a deal."

He looped the backpack over his shoulders, took off his hat, and shut the door.

"I can't believe you're actually leaving your hat in the truck."

"What can I say? I like to live on the edge."

I wiggled my brows. "Apparently."

He was only a few steps ahead of me, but it gave me just the chance I needed to do exactly what I should do, which was to check him out.

His broad shoulders filled out a black T-shirt, and his jeans hugged his thick thighs and trim waist perfectly. It was hard not to picture what he might look like under all that fabric.

As if he read my mind, he turned around and smiled. "You keeping up?"

"Just enjoying the view," I hummed.

"Aren't I the one who should be saying that?" he joked, waiting for me to catch up to him.

"We're equals in the world, right? I got to the punch line first."

My heart thudded to a complete stop when he smiled at me. His gaze quickly ran up and down my body. I was glad I'd chosen some loose cargo pants and a long-sleeved tee, only because after everything I ate this morning, I needed all the help I could get.

My phone buzzed in my back pocket, and I slipped it out to see who was possibly texting.

I glanced at the screen and stopped walking. It was only half a message.

Did you mean to text me the name Jacob Miller? Because I saw that the real

I scowled at my screen. That was it.

The text just stopped right in the middle of a sentence. A very important sentence.

I groaned and glanced over at Jacob.

"Everything okay?" he asked, noticing I'd stopped walking along the trail.

"I don't know. My sister texted me, but only half came over." I held up my phone toward the sky and waved it around as if that would bring the rest of the letters to me.

"Is she okay? Do we need to go back?" he asked.

"No. It was just..."

I couldn't very well tell him the text was about him.

But what was she going to say?

She saw that a Jacob Miller escaped prison with a few other inmates, or he's wanted because he buried his wife in the back forty, or...

Jacob waved his hand in front of my face, and I shook my head. "Sorry. It's just my imagination acting up again."

"You okay?"

"Yeah. Let's keep going. I'm sure I'll hear more from her later."

"Are you sure? It looked like whatever she wrote to you really threw you."

"Okay. Fine." I pushed my phone in front of him. "I can't keep secrets, and if you're going to lead me out into the middle of nowhere to leave me for dead, I'd like to know now."

"Huh?" He read the text and bit his bottom lip.

If it didn't look so sexy, I'd be concerned that he was contemplating something because I was onto him.

Jacob let out a deep breath. "I think I know what she was going to say."

A squirrel skittered by, and I nearly jumped into Jacob's arms. Usually, I loved squirrels.

"Have you been on the news? Are you wanted?" I whispered as if the wildlife might have an opinion on the matter if they overheard.

"Are you sure you despise writing? Because I think you'd be really good at it." Jacob smiled, and my tummy tightened.

I didn't want to hear what he had to say. I didn't want to hear what my sister was going to text.

For the first time in years, I wanted to do nothing more than enjoy a leisurely stroll in the middle of nowhere with a perfectly handsome stranger.

I held up my hand. "How about you don't tell me anything until the fourth date?"

Jacob nodded. "I don't want you to hear it from your sister."

I smiled and shoved my phone back into my pocket. "Then I won't look at what she has to say until tomorrow. I like hanging out with you, Jacob. You've turned a really weird vacation into something I don't think I'll ever forget."

Jacob's smile only grew, and he nodded. "I'm looking forward to date four, so I promise to keep an eye on you."

"Yeah? Date four?" I asked, shaking my head. "What's happening on date four?"

And then I remembered my rules, and I suddenly felt like my body had taken flight.

Did he actually want to kiss me?

My body flushed, and I sucked in a quick breath as silence stayed between us.

"If you'll let me," he added, smiling.

I glanced around the trail where bright orange flowers dotted the edge and purple vines tangled with the grass.

Jacob pushed the sunglasses up, and his eyes stayed on mine.

I nodded. "Weren't rules made to be broken?"

Jacob's blue eyes turned fiery as he stepped toward me. "I thought you'd never ask."

He wrapped his arms around my waist and pulled me toward him as his lips slowly slid across mine.

There was no rush, only an easiness I'd craved. His first kiss was as tender as I felt when a little moan escaped my lips. My hands brushed up his chest until they rested on his shoulders, teasing the backpack straps. He pulled me a little tighter as my lips parted, and our kisses deepened.

Jacob tasted so sweet, and I never wanted this moment to end.

But almost as quickly as it happened, it stopped with Jacob letting go and taking a step back. My body ached for more kisses, more surprises, but my head knew better.

This was all a fantasy that in less than two weeks would be nothing more than a fun memory.

Fun.

That was all this was.

I smiled, trying not to look as dopey as I felt. "That

was fun."

"Yeah." He smiled coyly. "It was really fun."

Jacob looped his fingers through mine, and we started back on the trail again.

I snuck a look in his direction as he moved his sunglasses back over his eyes.

"Thanks for letting me kiss you early."

I laughed and squeezed his hand. "My pleasure."

Jacob squeezed my hand back. "My pleasure more."

"Yeah? Remember who won the breakfast contest? I'll win this one too. I had way more fun than you did." I laughed.

"Oh, yeah?" he asked, stopping again and pulling me into him. "You make it simple to be me. You make me wanna be me."

He shoved his sunglasses up again, and his eyes locked on mine.

My breath caught in my throat as the connection between us only grew.

"Who else would you want to be, Jacob?" I whispered as his mouth swept over mine.

CHAPTER TEN

Jacob

Words ran through my mind at a pace I couldn't even keep up with.

Stealing the hard times away from me, reminding me of who I want to be.

Trading my bad days for good ones.

You make it simple to be me. You make me wanna be me.

All I want to do is steal you for me and memorize all the little things you do.

But you're my baby because you make it simple to be me.

I stared at the words that I'd managed to capture and closed my eyes as the music filled my veins. All I could think about was Lana's lips against mine, and then more words just flooded my mind.

I wrote more and knew more words were coming as I thought about holding her so close.

A little cotton dress, and all I can do is think about tangling with you in bed all day.

You gave me dreams I didn't know I had, but now I want to share.

Loving you is the easiest thing to do.

You gave me the gift of loving me for me, without all the messy parts.

I opened my eyes as the music wound down in my mind, my knee bobbed, and more words came again.

I knew when I saw you on the stage, we could go our different ways.

We had different lives, but there are so many roads in this life, and I want you on mine. I want your dreams.

I want to catch you if you fall.

I want to hold you tight. If you just smile in my

direction,

I know we can grow a love like we never knew.

I wanna believe that we can go from this life to the next on the same road, together.

I let out a deep sigh and forced myself to go get a cup of coffee.

Lana would be here any second.

Somehow, the kiss opened all kinds of doors. The first one was spending the day at the lake from the comfort of my own dock.

I smiled at the thought and loved how things between us had sped up, but I knew we both knew that we were working on borrowed time.

She had an inn to run, and I had something to do too.

I just didn't know what yet, but it felt like with her around, I might figure it out sooner than I thought.

I laughed and shook my head as I glanced around the kitchen. How could one female completely turn my world upside down and then show me she was the only one who could turn it right side up again?

Instead of writing lyrics, I should have been

emptying the containers of food I'd picked up at the store earlier.

But since I ran into Lana, life was new again. It was like I was hovering over this thing called life, taking everything in from a new angle. It was as if I could experience all the old details like they were new again, all because of Lana.

The thought made my pulse quicken and a rush of adrenaline cruise through me all because I couldn't wait to see her again.

I'd offered to pick her up at the hotel, but she said she wanted to walk around the lake. Truthfully, my house was easy to spot. The log home wasn't exactly carved out of humble pie, but I didn't build it. I just bought it from the original owners, and in my defense, there wasn't much on the market.

I glanced out the kitchen window and didn't see any sign of her yet, which was perfect since I hadn't even showered yet. I dumped the vegetables onto the plate and spooned the dip into a bowl and took off toward the bedroom.

Quickly turning on the water, I stripped and

climbed inside the shower, feeling the hot water roll down my skin. I quickly soaped up and watched the suds slide down the drain as I thought about Lana.

Where was this all leading? Could there be something more?

Four dates seemed too soon to care.

I heard the doorbell ring through my alarm system and quickly turned off the shower, grabbed a towel, and tried to dry off while pulling my jeans on as I headed toward the door.

Right when I got there, she'd already started to turn away.

I swung the door open.

"You don't let the grass grow under your feet," I teased.

Lana stopped and spun around with a smile replacing the worry that I briefly caught in her gaze. Her eyes widened when her gaze swept across my body.

"I had to pull on some pants. This morning got away from me, and I thought I should hop in the shower."

She still didn't say anything. The silence was killing me.

When her lips parted, I finally took a breath.

"You know what I learned in the last twenty-four hours?" Lana asked, smiling.

"What's that?" I leaned against the door.

"That I don't like rules."

I crossed my arms over my chest and smiled. "Like what?"

She pulled herself up to me and brushed a kiss across my mouth. Her slender fingers skated across my bare chest, and I instantly hardened.

Lana stepped closer and looked into my eyes. "Your house is beautiful."

"Thanks."

The heat rolling between us made me reconsider our date on the lake, but I knew I still needed to take things slow with Lana. Just because I got a kiss on date three instead of four didn't exactly set the stage for much else.

"Can you put a shirt on?" she joked. "You're really distracting."

My brows rose. "Yeah?"

"Oh, yeah. I'll be paddling in circles if you don't figure out something to pull over your head."

I chuckled as she walked under my raised arm as I closed the front door.

She spun around the large foyer that opened right into the large family room that overlooked the lake. The architects made sure just about all rooms had a view of the water, which I appreciated.

"Had I known you had such a great view, maybe I would have rented a room here." She eyed me. "Is that what you do?"

"What? Nightly rentals?" I shook my head. "I don't think I like people enough to do that."

Lana giggled. "I don't think you're supposed to stay in the house when you do that."

"Well, right off the bat, I would have screwed up." I motioned toward the family room, which tied directly into the kitchen. "I'll go grab a shirt, but you can help yourself to anything in the kitchen."

"Thanks." She smiled and nodded. "You know, I almost read my sister's text. I even started a new thread to her so I wouldn't break my promise."

Those words were all it took. I knew I'd found someone special, and I had absolutely no idea how to convince her that whatever was on the horizon for us was meant to be. I slipped a plaid shirt on and began buttoning it as I made my way to the kitchen, where she was munching on carrots.

I laughed. "Okay, I have to ask. What's with the carrots?"

She chuckled as her cheeks flushed. "You know how I'm pale?"

I shook my head. "I didn't really notice your being like Casper, no."

"Well, when I was a kid, I'd read that if you eat enough carrots, you get some color."

When I looked at her, I realized she was serious.

"I think you have to eat a lot of carrots to get that orange beta-carotene cast you're talking about."

"Orange?"

I nodded. "It's more of an orange hue, yeah."

Her brows shot up. "So, it's true?"

I laughed. "Yeah, I suppose."

She grinned and tossed a carrot toward me. "I was only teasing. I just like the crunch. Carrots have been my favorite since I was a kid."

I stared at Lana. "I totally believed you about wanting a tan."

Lana rolled her eyes and chuckled. "Gullible much?"

"Only around you, I think."

She pointed at me. "I held up my end of the bargain. I didn't peek."

Her words froze me in place. I knew what she was going to ask next.

"Are you going to tell me or make me drag it out of you?"

I watched Lana and memorized every single thing about this moment. I inhaled her carefree spirit, her ability to poke fun at me, her innocence and unjaded expectations.

Because it would all change the moment that she learned what I did for a living.

It always did.

I took a few steps toward her and leaned against

the island where I'd put the food out.

"You might need another carrot."

"Really?" She grabbed one and took a bite.

"First of all, I don't fault you for having terrible taste in music."

"Pardon me?" She took another bite.

"Remember yesterday when you mentioned you weren't too keen on some guy's music?"

"Yeah. What about it?"

"That guy was me."

She stared at me with absolutely no idea what I was talking about.

"I'm that guy. I'm the one who needs to pop some happy pills."

Lana's mouth parted.

Then it closed.

Then it opened.

Her hands slid up to her face, and she covered it completely as she started to spin in circles.

"Oh, no. Oh, no. Oh, no. I'm so sorry. Oh, no." She stopped herself and dropped her hands away from her face. "You're a songwriter?"

I pressed my lips together and nodded. "And singer."

"Wait. What?" She scowled.

"Look up Jacob Miller."

"You..." She stomped her foot. "Wait. You're a country singer?"

I scratched my chin. "Well, I've been telling you I wasn't a rodeo star."

Lana stared at me in shock, and I couldn't tell if it was the good kind or the bad kind.

It was usually the latter.

When I couldn't take the silence any longer, I took a step forward.

"Does that change things?" I reached for a carrot, hoping for some common ground.

She snatched it out of my fingers and took a bite.

"A few things." She let out an agitated sigh. "I hadn't planned on sleeping with a musician, but I might make an exception."

Lana walked over to the lake and slid her hands down her sides. "Why didn't you just tell me?"

She turned around and waited for my answer.

"Would we have gotten to date four?" I asked.

Lana shook her head and sighed. "I don't know."

"The very first night I saw you, Lana..." I sucked in a breath. "You took my breath away. I didn't want to lose my chance."

She studied me. "I have to confess that I'm a little worried."

I took a few steps closer. "Tell me. Tell me everything. Ask me anything. I don't want to lose what we've had going."

"Will I just be another notch in your belt?" She folded her arms across her chest.

I shook my head. "That's never been where my head's at. No, correction. When I was eighteen to probably twenty-two, I was in a boy band, and I did indulge a little too much in the party scene." I watched her reaction, but I knew no matter what, I'd be honest. "You've heard my music. I'm too depressed to care about notches."

She chuckled and hugged herself. "What does this all mean?"

I shrugged. "I'm still Jacob, the wannabe cowboy."

"Kind of has a whole new meaning, though." She twisted her lips into a playful scowl. "Wait a second."

"What?"

"Do you realize what this means?"

I smiled. "I really don't at this point."

"I don't either." She laughed. "I was just hoping you'd come up with something. I'm kind of at a loss for words. I knew what I was getting into with you wasn't a long-term type of thing, but this just solidifies that."

Crushing words.

A blow of epic proportions.

"Why's that?" I asked softly.

"Um... you're a rock star. You don't have time to be tied down."

"About that..."

Her eyes stayed on mine. "Yeah?"

"The reason I'm here—"

"The *real* reason?"

I nodded. "Is because I told my manager that I'm done. I'm done with touring. I'm done with music. He thinks it's temporary, but I'm done."

"Then why were you lurking in a karaoke bar?" she asked.

Her question completely disarmed me. It was like she knew me better than I knew myself.

"I don't know."

"Because you love music," she answered.

I nodded.

"You don't have to make these overreaching, sweeping generalizations about your career. It's good that you didn't tell your manager what you're really thinking." She shook her head. "I don't think you're over it. You just might be looking for inspiration."

I smiled and nodded slowly. "And I think I might have found her."

CHAPTER ELEVEN

Lana

I was trying to play it cool. Oh, was I ever trying.

I kept my breathing at an even tempo. I didn't let him see me sweat.

No wonder Samantha kept texting. I wanted to pretend it didn't matter that I was standing in the kitchen of a man who'd been around the world touring sold-out stadiums while being picked on by yours truly for having too moody of music.

Jacob's eyes locked on mine, and my insides swirled.

I'd kissed a famous country star, and I'd lived to

tell about it.

Bringing in a deep breath, I let it out slowly. "I really like you."

"I like you too." He smiled, and it turned me to mush.

"I'm a simple girl. I don't have big, lofty dreams." I cleared my throat. "I mean, shoot. My idea of a vacation was going to a funeral."

Jacob grimaced and nodded. "At least it wasn't yours."

I chuckled nervously. "Yeah. That would be too long of a vacation, for sure."

Jacob smiled. "You okay with this info? It seems like you've kind of—"

I glanced around his expansive kitchen and beautiful view of the lake before turning back to him.

"Turned spastic?" I nodded, grinning. "Yeah. I'm just dandy."

"I can see through that smile of yours. I've seen enough of those kinds of smiles around to know you're not okay."

"You're as bad as my sister."

He gave a slight nod. "The writer?"

"Yup." I folded my arms over my chest. "I knew this thing between us was just for fun while I was in Montana."

"Then why does that have to change?" he asked.

I shrugged. "I don't know. Maybe it doesn't."

He walked toward me. "It doesn't. I'm still Jacob, the wannabe cowboy."

Seeing the earnest look in his eyes nearly killed me. He was pleading with me, and I wasn't even sure for what.

I liked him. I've had more fun with him than I've had with just about anyone, but I attributed a lot of it to the vacation. But there was a tiny little trickle of hope that maybe wanted to see if this could last a little longer than two weeks, and after that kiss, it was hard not to be spinning in a million different directions.

I smiled and trailed my finger along his chest. "My Hollywood cowboy."

His eyes stayed on mine. "Are you sure that's how you really feel? Because I wasn't the one eating all of Jaqueline's carrots."

"You're never going to let that go, are you?" I snickered and reached for a celery stick just to prove I could.

"I have a confession."

"Another one?" I braced myself on the counter. "I don't think I can handle too many more."

He laughed. "For the first time in years, I'm feeling inspired."

"Really?" I asked, surprised.

He nodded.

"Is it Montana?" I asked.

Jacob let out a deep breath and shook his head. "It was watching you on that stage. You were just having such a blast, bringing joy to people."

"Well, the people of this fine town can thank the cocktails." I shook my head, suddenly realizing he was serious. "Do you really want to give it all up?"

He nodded. "I'm just over it. The long days and even longer nights. Life is such a big party for so many of them, and all I wanted was to sing to make people happy."

"But you haven't been happy."

"Not recently. No."

I pressed my lips together and scowled. "Is that why your music is so... sad?"

He smiled. "You want to know what's crazy?"

"Kind of."

"I didn't know it was sad until you said something in the truck yesterday."

"Really?" It wasn't a secret. His songs were hauntingly beautiful, but the topics were deep and twisted and exhausting and... sad. It was why I always turned the station. There was too much angst rolled into a two-minute spot for me.

He nodded.

"Now that I know it's you behind the words, I just don't see that side of you."

"You bring out the best in me."

I smiled, feeling like that was the best compliment I could ever hear. "I feel the same."

He chuckled. "For the next ten days or so, we'll be feeling like we're on top of the world."

I laughed and nodded. "Yup. Until I head out to Washington."

"Nice."

"Can I ask you something?"

"Might as well."

"Why are so many of your songs so full of sadness? It seems like you've got it pretty good."

Granted, I thought that about my sister Samantha too, and all she'd wanted was to be considered normal and be accepted by her family. I should know by now that money didn't cure all ails.

"I'll have to think about that and give you a really good answer." He poured himself some sparkling water. "The short answer is I never stopped long enough to know, but I'll tell you when I figure it out."

I smiled, content with his answer for now. "The older I get, the more I realize that appearances aren't everything. In fact, most of the time, they are just that."

Jacob tilted his head slowly.

"Have you ever noticed that? People always worry what they look like to others, fishing around for information, wanting to compare themselves to you or someone else they know rather than just being content."

"And you pride yourself on being content, right?" It was more of a statement.

I chuckled. "Well, I thought I was, but I'm in the middle of Montana, unsure whether I really want to go back to Washington."

The answer looked like it surprised him. "I'm that fun?"

I laughed. "Surprisingly, yes."

"My profession is all about appearances," he confessed.

"Is that why you're so attached to the hat?" I asked. "For the record, you're the sexiest man I've ever seen in one."

He laughed. "I'm attached to the hat because nine times out of ten, I can pull it down, and nobody recognizes me."

I nodded. "Does it get old?"

I thought back to the group of teenage girls surrounding him the first night I'd arrived in Montana.

"It can be. Sometimes, though, it's a wonderful

reminder."

"Of what?"

"That I'm not all I'm cracked up to be."

I waved my hands at him. "Oh, please. You're all that and a bowl of macaroni and cheese."

"Thanks. I'll have to remember that."

I glanced around his beautiful home. "Do you really need reminders that you're pretty great? Your songwriting and voice got you all this."

"That's a skill, but what about as a person?" His eyes sparkled with something I couldn't quite put my finger on. "As a person, what have I done for myself? I have no family, not many in the way of close friends. I spent more holidays in a hotel room than I'd like to admit."

"You know what's interesting?"

"What?"

"My sister dealt with something similar. We all thought she had everything anyone could ever want, but we were wrong."

He let out a deep breath. "How'd she fix it?"

I laughed. "She got married."

"Ah, just like that."

I chuckled and wiggled my brows. "No pressure. In all seriousness, our family has been a work in progress for quite some time, but things kind of came into focus for all of us. If you're starting to feel like things need to change, I fully believe you can make it happen. It just takes knowing what you want first."

He laughed. "How are you doing on that one?"

I stood on my toes and planted a kiss on his lips. "Not terribly well. I came to Montana to find myself, and I'm more confused than ever."

And it was true. I'd always been the content sister, the daughter who'd always been calm and levelheaded. It had always been that way. Between my sisters and me, everyone knew that I would just go with the flow. Samantha was the one with the adventurous spirit. Vera was the feisty one. My mom even painted doors to commemorate each of us. Mine was blue. Vera's was red, and Samantha's was yellow. Cloudberry Inn still had those doors, and I'd never change them.

A smile touched my lips as I thought about my

mom and the woman she was, even if I only knew the side she'd wanted us to see.

What I saw now was a courageous and brave woman who overlooked a loneliness that I couldn't even imagine.

"I tend to do that to people." He smiled and rested his arms on my shoulders. "Is your family close? It seems like you all are."

I let out a deep breath. "Yes and no."

Jacob laughed. "There is never a simple answer with you, is there?"

I laughed and shook my head. "My mom passed away eight years ago. For the first seven, Samantha, Vera, and I weren't very close, as I've mentioned. Sam lived in New York, and even though Vera was my sidekick at the inn, we barely spoke. When Samantha came back into our lives again, life felt right." I looked into his eyes. "That feeling didn't last long, though."

"Why's that?"

I took a step back, and his arms dropped to his sides.

"I always had this vision of my parents. I thought

they were the epitome of what love looked like, and then I found out I had a secret sister. My dad wasn't faithful to my mom. Worse yet, it was when my mom was pregnant. Even crazier is that I knew the girl. She was my sister's best friend."

"Wow. That's a lot."

I nodded. "And it all came to light in the last six months or so. It kind of blew everything up for me. I'd always wanted the relationship that my parents had, and then I found out they didn't even have it." I shrugged, feeling the gnawing feeling in my gut again when I thought about my dad. "My dad doesn't even know."

Jacob shook his head. "What do you mean?"

"My half-sister is Charlotte. Anyway, her mom didn't want anyone to know she was pregnant with my dad's child, even him. Charlotte's mom didn't want to tear someone's family apart. Although, the act of sleeping with him kind of did that."

"He doesn't know he has a fourth daughter?" Jacob's eyes stayed focused on mine, and I suddenly had a lump in my throat.

It was crazy. I hadn't cried about any of this.

Ever.

And now, all of a sudden, I wanted to shed a hurricane full of tears. Between Lars and Charlotte, I was a mess.

"What is it about Montana?" I sniffled. "This place keeps making me cry about things that I'd never normally cry about."

"Maybe you've become an expert at keeping your feelings locked inside."

I smiled and nodded. "I think you're right about that."

"I have my moments."

I glanced toward the lake, sliding my phone on the counter. "Should we head out?"

Jacob nodded. "Might as well. We can just go out this door to the back."

"Awesome." I followed Jacob out the door when he stopped and turned to look at me.

"Is someone going to tell your dad?" he asked.

I nodded. "Yeah. Charlotte wanted to be the one who did, but she keeps chickening out. My dad lives in Arizona, so I can understand her wanting to do it in person."

"I just know how I'd feel if I found out I had a daughter I didn't know about."

"And in your profession..." I grimaced, and he chuckled.

"Safety first."

I rolled my eyes and blushed.

We walked over to a stand where several kayaks and canoes were on display.

"This is a pretty fancy setup."

"Came with the house."

I smiled as he tossed me a life jacket. "What's this?"

"Safety first," he repeated and laughed while he put his own on.

"Fine, but I want you to know for the record that I was a diving champion in junior high."

"I'll remember that if I lose anything at the bottom of the lake."

I scowled and glanced down at the outfit I'd so carefully picked out. To fit in with Jacob's cowboy theme, I'd tied a plaid shirt at my waist with a pair of denim shorts. After the kiss yesterday, I'd made sure to leave the buttons undone more than usual. Since I didn't really have any cleavage to display, I'd hoped that skin would do the trick, and now I had to cover up.

He reached for a green canoe and walked it down the dock like it was nothing more than a bag of groceries.

I looked down at my orange life jacket and realized it was as good as it was gonna get as I traipsed down the dock after him.

"Ready?" he asked as I nodded and looked out toward the beautiful reflection bouncing off the water. I pulled the sunglasses out of my back pocket and slipped them on as he did the same.

"This is breathtaking." I scanned the lake and shook my head. "I can see why you don't want to leave."

Jacob smiled and nodded. "Not as breathtaking as you."

CHAPTER TWELVE

Jacob

I knew there was so much more to her story about her sisters, but I didn't want to overstep my bounds. She stopped talking and changed the subject.

Even though things were moving fast, we both knew that her vacation would come to an end sooner than either of us planned. Maybe she just didn't feel like opening up all the way to a near stranger.

Stranger.

The word sounded foreign. I didn't think of myself as a stranger, and I certainly didn't think of Lana as one. In fact, I felt closer to her in these last few days than I had with anyone.

Lana bounded toward me on the dock, and it took everything I had not to let the canoe go with my foot and kiss her.

So instead of doing that, I gave her a cheesy one-liner about how beautiful she was, but it was true. I just didn't understand why whenever she was around, these things just spewed out of my mouth like I was Rico Suave.

She winked at me. "You're not too shabby yourself. Now, let's get paddling."

I couldn't help but smile as her carefree spirit overtook my own. After years of writing words that made my heart hurt but felt so cathartic, I suddenly couldn't even pull ten words together that would make me feel that way any longer.

Nodding, I took her hand, and she climbed into the canoe without incident. We were off to a good start. I grabbed the oars and stepped into the canoe.

As I congratulated myself for starting this adventure off like a pro, the canoe started to wobble.

Lana let out a shriek, and the entire canoe flipped

over. Before I had a chance to panic, Lana's head popped out of the water with a fit of laughter erupting from her soul as I reached for a rogue oar.

She treaded water and shook her head. "I didn't know the reason I needed the life jacket is because you suck at water sports."

"That was a complete fluke."

"Okay, Cowboy." She grinned coyly.

Without another thought, I swam toward her and pulled her into my arms.

"Was this all part of your plan?" she whispered, looking into my gaze.

"I'm not this good of a planner."

Her doe eyes were hooded with the same desire running through my veins. It didn't matter that the lake water was cold. The heat was building between us at an unstoppable pace.

She raised her wet arms out of the water and looped them over my neck.

This was heaven, feeling her legs brush up against mine.

"You know, we could get a lot closer if someone

didn't insist on these life jackets."

I rested my forehead on hers as our bodies stayed distant, but all it took was a rogue leg to swipe against mine to make me want to take her back to my house.

"So, now what?" she asked. "I didn't bring a change of clothes."

Water dripped down her cheeks, and I brushed the droplets off.

"We could dry off in the sun or—"

She cut me off and nodded. "I'm never one to give up. Perseverance is my middle name."

With that, she took a little swim toward the canoe, and my hopes were dashed as I watched her swing her leg over the canoe seamlessly.

Then it hit me. "Wait a second. You got into that canoe like a pro."

She looked down at me in the water as I continued to tread.

"Who, me?" She feigned innocence, and I shook my head.

"I wasn't the one who made the canoe go over, was I?"

Lana slid her tongue across her bottom lip. "I don't know what you're implying, Cowboy."

She handed me one end of a paddle and led me over to the dock. "But, I also spent a lot of time at Lake Whatcom."

I hoisted myself into the canoe and eyed her. "You're just full of surprises."

"Only the good kind."

I grinned and pushed us off with my paddle when terror darted through me.

My phone.

I slid it out of my pocket, and it was dead. Not a little dead.

Dead. Dead.

When Lana turned around to see why I'd stopped paddling, her mouth dropped open.

"Oh, no. I'm so sorry." Her eyes widened. "I had no idea. I thought you would have left it at the house."

"So, it was planned." I eyed her suspiciously.

"I'm so sorry." She chewed on her bottom lip, which only made her look even cuter.

"No worries. My manager has been texting me

nonstop. Now I have an excuse not to answer him. You're just full of good luck for me."

She smiled, looking only somewhat relieved. "I'm glad you see it that way."

"It's the only way I see it."

We paddled deeper onto the open lake. A few houses could be spotted along the shoreline, but the lake wasn't that busy, probably because it was a weekday.

"I just have to say it one more time." She stopped paddling and turned around on the bench. "I'm sorry."

I laughed and shook my head. "I promise you. It's no big deal. It backs up automatically. I'll just order one this week."

She didn't start paddling again. Instead, she put her paddle down and spun on the bench with barely a wobble.

Her clothes were still damp and stuck to her body. I was beginning to wish I hadn't made her wear a life jacket.

"I have a question." Her eyes stayed on mine.

"I hope I have an answer."

"Someone like you, who has it all, who's probably done it all..." She looked toward the pines arching along the lakefront. "Do you ever wonder if there's something more to life?"

Her question socked me right in the gut as I nodded slowly. "It's what I think about every day."

She nodded, reaching for my knee. "You've accomplished so much and have the same question that I have, and I haven't even done anything. Does that mean we'll never get an answer?"

Her words were like shrapnel, and I shook my head frantically. "What do you mean you haven't done anything? You've run a successful inn. You're a kind person. You have a solid family life."

She let out a heavy sigh. "It wasn't all that successful until my sister helped out. I don't think business is my strong suit."

Lana's gaze fell to the bottom of the canoe. "The truth of the matter is the only reason I really reached out to my sister was that the inn was in trouble, and I knew she could help... financially."

I saw the confession tearing her up inside.

"And she has helped, from the sounds of it."

Lana brought her gaze up to mine. "I let seven years go by over pettiness, and then she was there in an instant when we needed help."

"That doesn't make you a bad person. It's what families are for."

Lana didn't look convinced.

I put the paddle down and reached for her hands. "Tell me this."

Her eyes stayed on mine.

"It's a family business, right?"

She nodded. "My dad left it to us when he took off to Arizona."

"Once her writing career took off, did she help you out?"

Lana chuckled. "Her career took off when she was like fifteen. Not really. She needed to focus on that."

"Maybe helping out now is her way of giving back."

Lana smiled. "That's what she says, but I've got a serious guilt complex. The kicker is that when she got to the inn, I didn't even want to bring anything up."

LEAVING YOU

I nodded, watching Lana torture herself over something her sister probably hadn't even thought twice about.

"Listen, if your sister didn't want to help, she wouldn't have. Maybe she needed a change from just writing? I know how many things I've missed out on with my career. It's not that I'm not grateful. I'm just ready for the next chapter."

Lana's lips finally started to turn in the right direction. "She does seem to love being at Cloudberry."

"And it sounds like if you hadn't invited her to the inn, she never would have met the man she fell in love with and married."

Lars popped into my head.

"Do you know what's really weird?" she asked, pushing her sunglasses onto her head.

"Besides your deliberately tipping us over in the canoe?"

"Yeah, besides that." She grinned, squinting at me. "Not only is this a vacation, but it's also like the world's best therapy session."

I smiled and nodded. "I know what you mean, except that you're prettier than any therapist I've been to."

Surprise dashed through her gaze. "You've been to therapy?"

I nodded. "Loads of it."

I wanted to suddenly tell her everything about my family. What we'd been through.

About my sister.

But this was her vacation.

Lana nodded. "I could probably use a lot of it. I've often lain in bed and gone over what I'd tell a therapist if I spoke to one."

That surprised me.

She smiled. "The list is long."

"You seem so happy." I watched her take a deep breath. "Even when you're sad."

Lana laughed. "Years of practice. Being in the hospitality industry forces a person to put on a smile and make things right."

I nodded, wondering how in all my years meeting people, I'd never met someone quite like Lana. She was strong, independent, funny, charming, positive, happy, and made me feel challenged.

She stretched her legs as our canoe continued to float in the middle of the lake.

"I like strawberry ice cream and listening to eighties music." Her eyes focused on mine. "It's a lot perkier than what you tend to sing about."

Did I mention her honesty because it was quite unlike anything I'd encountered before? It was refreshing and disarming.

"I'll have to remember that if I make a playlist for us."

"Aw. That would be sweet." She touched her heart. "It's weird to think that I'm sitting in the middle of a lake with a man more famous than most anyone—"

"Except you didn't know who I was," I added.

"Don't get your feelings hurt. I think I'm permanently stuck in every era but my own." She grinned. "Anyway, it's just weird that all of these things have transpired because someone I used to know passed away."

I nodded, not wanting to say the wrong thing. Her gaze looked like it held so much more.

"Almost cosmic in a sense, and I'm not even sure I believe in any of that." Her hand brushed mine, and electricity bolted through me. If I weren't worried about tipping the canoe over, I would have kissed her again.

"The world seems to have made our encounter seamless." I sucked in a breath as more lyrics filled my head.

Dropping my gaze to Lana's, I wondered what she'd think if she knew I had so many songs I suddenly wanted to write for her.

"Are you sure I couldn't get you to sing karaoke again? Any eighties song you want? More pink squirrels?" I grinned, hoping I could convince her of how well she sang and how desperate I was to hear her again.

"Only if someone's life depended on it," she teased.

I nodded. "I get it. I get it."

As the boat bobbed gently, I noticed the sun

throwing a golden hue across her green eyes. She was absolutely gorgeous.

"Have you ever had any serious relationships?" she asked, jarring me right out of the serenity I'd landed in.

I shook my head urgently to get the point across. "No. I wouldn't call any of my relationships serious."

Lana twisted her lips into a perplexed look. "Maybe I should rephrase my question. Have you had a long-term relationship?"

I laughed and nodded. "I see what you did there."

She winked at me. "I've always admired your quickness."

"Well, I have found myself in some tricky situations."

"With relationships?" She looked far too intrigued to have this go well.

"Yeah."

"Go on." She motioned with her hands, leaning forward. "Your secrets are safe with me."

I thought about how to say it. I knew it wouldn't come out right.

"I've been set up more times than I'd like to count. Usually, it's some PR fiasco I didn't see coming. Other times, I lend out my house and realize after the fact that it looks like I invited her to move in when in actuality, I just thought since I was gone anyway..." I shrugged. "What does it matter if she lives there? I won't be there to see her."

Lana whistled as her expression vacillated between horror and humor.

"Would I call any of my encounters long-term? No. I'm always on the road. Would I call them relationships? Eh, maybe?"

She laughed and nodded. "Well, I appreciate your honesty, but I think I'm more confused now than before I asked you."

"What about you?" he asked.

"My inn has been my other half for well over a decade," she teased. "Except for the occasional skinny dip in the pool with the bellboy or gardener, I'd say my love life is pretty nonexistent."

Lana watched me closely as she gauged my reaction. I wasn't going to judge. I'd been around more than I'd like to admit.

The words finally came to me. "It sounds like we're both students of keeping things casual."

She nodded. "Yeah. Casual. I like how that sounds."

CHAPTER THIRTEEN

Lana

"You're telling me that you've kissed *the* Jacob Miller, as in the country singer superstar?" Samantha nearly hyperventilated on the other end of the phone.

"A few times," I confessed.

"And?" My sister sounded completely exasperated.

"He's a good kisser."

"How could you keep this from me? Wait until Vera finds out. You know he's her favorite singer, right?"

"You're kidding." I hadn't the faintest clue.

"Nope."

I tucked my leg under me as I stared out my hotel room window, speakerphone on, half-eaten waffles on the table, and only the gorgeous lake separating me from Jacob.

"This is going to sound completely crazy, but when I saw he was in town..." My sister sucked in a breath so loud it made the phone crackle. "I just had this feeling you'd bump into him."

"Well, I bumped into him, all right, and I sang Nancy Sinatra at karaoke, drank something called a pink squirrel, and dumped Jacob into the lake on a canoe ride."

"You're never going to want to come back to the inn."

"I actually miss the inn." It was hard to believe the words were rolling off my tongue, but it was true.

There was comfort in knowing that through everything our family had experienced, the inn still stood, welcoming people and letting them escape the everyday, which helped me escape too.

"Tell me this," Samantha continued, not really

focusing on much else other than Jacob Miller.

"Is he as cute as he looks on television?" she asked.

"I hope Garrett's not in the room."

Samantha snickered. "He's right next to me."

I chuckled. "He's even better-looking in person."

I didn't want to reveal that I thought he was some tech guru playing pretend cowboy on vacation or that he helped wipe my tears at Lars's funeral, or that I was quickly falling for someone who was an impossibility.

She sighed. "I was afraid of that. Just be careful."

I chuckled. "So far, we've been horseback riding, hiking on a trail, and canoeing on a lake. I think I'll be just fine."

"Do you still plan on driving back in a week and a half or whenever it was?" she asked.

"Yup." The thought actually made my belly tense. Instinctively, I knew this fun little vacation fling that wasn't quite a fling had no potential. He'd get back to his life, and I'd get back to the inn.

"Well, I thought it would be fun if I flew out there

and drove back with you. Would you be game?"

"Really?"

"Yeah."

"Wait a second. Is this so you can meet the cowboy?"

"No. I swear I'd come up with this idea with Garrett a couple of days ago."

I chuckled. "Well, whatever the case, I think that would be awesome, but who'll run the inn?"

"It's only a couple of days, and Amy will be just fine. Her sisters can help out. She already checked with them."

I smiled, feeling a little less stressed about leaving Montana. It would be fun to have a sisterly road trip back to Cloudberry. It would help me forget who and what I was leaving behind.

"You didn't tell me about Lars's memorial service," she continued. "How was it"

"Sad."

Samantha laughed. "Thank you for that, Captain Obvious."

I chuckled and shook my head as I stared across

the lake. "No, I mean sadder than I expected, but for a different reason."

"What's the reason?" Samantha asked.

"It's hard to explain." I sighed. "But it was almost like everyone there showed up as a formality. I don't know. It really made me sad. I think he lived a hard life."

"I'm sorry, Lana. That's tough to see."

"But I'm glad I came." I thought back to the tears I'd shed. "I couldn't stop tearing up, and I still don't even know why. I think it scared me to see such little growth from someone I knew so young."

"That would make sense."

"I don't know. It was a lot to process." I caught a glimpse of Jacob walking across the lawn and smiled. "But I'm glad I made the trek. It showed me that I was genuinely okay with where I was at in life."

"Especially now that you're dating a country superstar?"

I laughed and shook my head. "I think the word *dating* is a little presumptuous. He and I know this can go nowhere."

"How many times have you seen him?" my sister asked.

"This will be the fifth time."

"Five dates?" Samantha sounded impressed. "Think about it. Most people, when they first meet someone, go out on one date a week at first. In a way, it's almost like you've been going out with him for five weeks."

I laughed and shook my head. "Food for thought with that one, Sam."

"I bet you know him better than you realize."

I liked that idea and couldn't help but smile. I'd lost sight of Jacob several minutes ago, so when the thump on my hotel door rattled into the room, I couldn't help but feel pure giddiness.

"Oh, that's him. I've gotta go."

Samantha squealed into the phone. "Good luck on date five. Just remember what I said."

"Love ya."

"You too."

I hung up the phone and made my way over to the door where Jacob stood with two coffees.

"How did you get these so fast? I just saw you walking around the lake. You are a gift from heaven." I inhaled the steam from the lid and closed my eyes.

"That rough of a morning, huh?" he teased

I blinked my eyes open. "Every morning is that rough of a morning. The sun and I don't see eye to eye until at least ten o'clock, which is kind of ironic since I've run an inn for ages and had to get up when it was dark most mornings."

Jacob nodded. "I'm not a real fan of early mornings. Every so often, I like to do it just to prove I can, but I'd rather wake up when I'm ready."

I laughed. "We have a couple of new hires at the inn, and one of them works early so she can pick her kids up, and I'm forever grateful to her." I stepped back from the door and waved inside. "Did you want to come in?"

"Sure." He took a few steps inside and smiled. "You're not as tidy as I thought."

I scowled at him and looked around the room as I set my coffee cup down. "I thought this was clean."

Granted, I had a few articles of clothing falling

from the suitcase, but I had all my dirties in a bag in the corner, the magazines I'd collected piled on the table next to my phone, my snack bags neatly lined up on the dresser, and—

My eyes widened, and I darted to the black bra that proudly dangled from the closet handle, followed by a pair of granny panties crumpled right below it.

A squeal rolled off my lips as I fought with the elastic of the bra straps that magically tangled around the handle as my foot kicked the underwear into the closet.

Except that it got stuck on the toe of my shoe and flipped right off the end and floated in the air.

"Nooo." I screeched as the cotton fabric flew slowly in the air, arching ever so gracefully toward the country singer's head.

I snapped the bra strap right off the closet and dove toward Jacob, who managed to catch the underwear with his left hand while I tackled him like a quarterback.

"You know, this isn't the first time I've had a woman throw her underwear at me," he said wryly, trying to catch us both.

His arms wrapped around me to steady us, and my heart skipped a beat. The bed was only a foot or two away, and there was a part of me that wished we'd landed on it.

Snatching the underwear from his fingers, I marched to my dirty laundry bag and stuffed them in.

"Well, good for you." I rolled my eyes, and he laughed.

"I'm glad you find this so amusing." I grinned, unable to even pretend to be mad at him.

"What I find amusing is that your hotel room happens to look like my tour bus."

"Right? I'm on vacation. It's not like expected anyone to come in." I grinned.

"At least I got to hold you this morning, as brief as it was." He took a sip of coffee as my heart fluttered wildly.

I straightened and nodded. "It was a nice way to start the day."

"Wasn't it?" He grinned and glanced toward the lake.

"What do you have planned for me today?" I teased.

We hadn't talked about doing anything in particular today, other than meeting up, and here he was, and I was starting to miss him already, which made no sense since he was standing right in front of me.

"It's a surprise."

"A good surprise?" I asked.

"This one could go either way," he confessed.

"Uh. That's not really selling it." I took a sip of the coffee and reveled in the taste.

"It's a little outside the box, but I thought it would be a great way for you to see Montana and maybe fall in love with it." His blue eyes stayed on mine as I took another sip.

"I already love Montana."

"But not enough to extend your trip," he pointed out. "You're leaving in like nine days?"

I nodded, surprised he was counting down the days too. "My sister's actually going to come out a day or two early, and we're going to drive back together.

It should be fun."

He smiled but didn't say anything.

Instead, it felt like all the oxygen got sucked right out of the room. I took a deep breath, but it didn't help at all. I almost felt like I was gasping for air.

And the way he was looking at me stirred so many emotions inside me.

Jacob touched my cheek. "I'll tell you this, though. If we get there and you want to back out, I'm okay with it."

My eyes widened as his words brought me back to reality.

"Should I be worried?" I asked.

"Do you mind heights?"

"I don't give it much thought." I shrugged. "But I generally enjoy keeping both feet firmly on the ground."

He nodded. "Okay. We'll see then."

I looked down at my jeans, T-shirt, and sneakers. "Will this work?"

"That should work, and you look great, like always."

I smiled at the flattery. "That will always go a long way with me."

"What?" he asked, shaking his head.

"Praise." I grinned. "I'm kind of like a puppy dog in that regard."

He patted my head, and I laughed.

"See? I like that." I grabbed my phone before we headed out for the day's adventure, and I wondered what in the world he had in store for us.

I also wondered how hard it would be to leave, and if I'd ever look back and wish I'd stayed a little longer.

As we made our way through the lobby, a few people timidly walked over to Jacob for a picture or two and an autograph. When he was finished, he turned back to me, looking somewhat sheepish, which only made me like him more.

It was funny. If I'd seen this guy on television performing or being interviewed, I would have completely dismissed him as a pretty face, probably too cocky to have a conversation with, and completely detached from the world. He was the opposite of any of that.

He reached for my hand and squeezed it as we walked to the parking lot.

"You know, I'm growing kind of fond of you." He glanced at me sideways, and I couldn't help but smile.

"Given enough time, I'm sure I could screw that up," I joked.

"I'd be pretty surprised if you could."

We slowed as we got closer to the truck, and I nodded as he let go of my hand.

"This whole thing seems crazy, doesn't it?" I asked.

"You mean our meeting?"

I nodded. "Yeah. Just everything."

"Maybe it's not as crazy as we think."

Smiling, I hopped into the truck only to have him already sitting in the driver's seat with the truck running and in reverse.

"Are you going back to San Francisco anytime soon?" I asked, sneaking a peek in his direction.

Jacob shook his head. "No. I've already signed with a broker. It's going to be listed in a few weeks when they're done staging it or whatever they insist on doing."

"Wow. So, you'll really be a Montana guy?"

He let out a deep breath and tapped the wheel. "Yeah."

"You seem nervous about it."

"Nah." Jacob shook his head. "It's the best decision I've ever made."

"How do you know? How are you so certain?" I asked, genuinely curious. "I wanted to be that certain in life. I wanted to know for a fact that I never wanted to leave Cloudberry. I wanted to know something in my life for certain, but it never happened."

Jacob smiled and looked over at me. "I got to meet you."

A blush crept over me, and I smiled. "You're really good at that."

"At what?"

"Knowing what to say."

"Only to you." He grinned, giving me a quick glance.

I didn't want to take the moment too seriously.

After all, how could anything this quick be so serious?

"Tell me then," I continued. "How do you know for certain that giving up everything you've worked for and selling your place in the city and hiding away in Montana is the right thing?"

Jacob smiled and nodded slowly. "It's just a feeling, Lana. I don't know how to explain it other than to say that my mind and body are in complete agreement that this is where I want to be, what I want to do."

"And if you're wrong?"

He shrugged and pulled in toward some kind of field. "Then I'm wrong. It's not the end of the world. Change can be good, and it's never that bad."

I laughed nervously and looked toward him in surprise. "I wouldn't know, but what is this place?"

"It's a heliport."

I was sure my eyes grew twice their size. "As in helicopter?"

"Yup." He nodded and parked his truck on the gravel drive.

"I didn't know there was an airfield here."

"It's private." He looked at the clock radio. "And our helicopter should be arriving any minute."

My heart started beating quickly as I thought about going up in the air with nothing but a large blade spinning us toward the sky.

"You can back out," he said softly.

I saw a little dot in the sky become bigger as it came closer to the field.

"No. I need to do this." I smiled, feeling the knot in my stomach give way to something much greater.

A sense of freedom from the everyday.

"You feel that certainty in your gut?" Jacob asked.

I smiled and nodded slowly. "I do. It was a gradual process. Started as a tiny knot and gave way to something kind of hopeful."

He grinned. "The joy of the unexpected."

"I like that."

The helicopter landed, and Jacob looked over at me.

"You ready to see Montana the way I first did?"

I happily nodded and slid out of the truck. The sky's vivid blue looked as if it went on forever.

Jacob slid his hand over mine, and we made our way to the helicopter, where one of the pilots greeted us while reminding us to stay low.

The swooshing of the blade was exhilarating, but not nearly as much as when we got buckled in, headphones on, and lift off began.

The experience was absolutely nothing like a plane as we lifted off the ground. It felt as if we were cutting into the sky as we flew higher, and the noise increased steadily.

Excitement pulsed through me as I looked down to see the emerald trees as thick as a quilt patchworked with the beauty of the deep-blue waters and town.

It suddenly felt like anything was possible. I looked over at Jacob, who wasn't looking out of the helicopter. He was watching me. I didn't know what to make of the feeling rushing through me, but I knew something was changing inside me.

Up here, the world had opened so wide below that I knew I was nothing more than an ant in the maze of life, but maybe for once, I wanted to construct that maze and make my own way. I just didn't know how.

CHAPTER FOURTEEN

Jacob

Seeing the thrill running through Lana's gaze brought enough happiness to last a lifetime. I swore the sight was the best thing I could ever experience.

With every sideways smile she threw at me, every nervous giggle and clammy palms, I knew this special moment we were sharing would stay with her even if nothing else between us did.

It wasn't that I believed we were in the midst of some whirlwind romance, but I firmly felt that there was something really important happening between us. The pull to her was too great to ignore, and getting to share these experiences stacked on top of one another only made me more certain that I needed to let myself believe there was some kind of future with her.

Lana turned her head away from the glass and smiled dopily in my direction with a dreamy look in her gaze.

Her voice carried into my headphones, and she sounded like an angel. "I never want to land."

I smiled and nodded. "It's beautiful, isn't it?"

"Thank you." Lana leaned her head against the cold glass and looked below, and I wanted to know more than anything what she was thinking about as she looked at the place that I now called home.

"You kind of outdid yourself with this one," she said, chuckling.

The moment I came up with the idea last night, I scrambled to charter a helicopter that would come out to Big Fork and pick us up, but like everything else with Lana, my plan fell into place perfectly.

"I tried." I slid my hand to her knee, and she put her hand on top of mine.

"You're making it essentially impossible for any other guy to compare. You know that, right?"

"That's the plan," I teased, but I was more than serious. "I figure as soon as you get on I-90, you'll forget about me unless I pull out all the stops."

She snickered and shook her head. "You had me with your little cowboy hat long ago."

I laughed, knowing our long ago was about five days out.

The pilot informed us that we'd be landing soon.

I saw the disappointment sprinkle through her gaze, which made me even happier since I'd planned an early dinner in town.

Lana turned to me and smiled. "You've made every day even more special than the last. Thank you."

I grinned, knowing the truth was that she'd done the same for me.

She looked out the window where a smattering of green conifers looked like a quilt edged along the water. The landscape traded out green for tan as we made our way back to the heliport.

I fully understood that whatever was happening

between Lana and me was temporary. We both knew it, but I wanted to make our time together count, maybe remind her how high the bar should be set for the next guy.

I smiled wickedly to myself.

As the chopper set down, she turned to me again. Her smile blinded me to the point of no return as we removed our headphones.

"I will never forget this." She drew a breath, and her eyes locked on mine.

The heat between us fired to an intensity I'd never felt before, but there were two men sitting in the cockpit, so it was short-lived.

The copilot climbed out of the front and opened the back for us, giving us instructions as we kept our heads down, held hands, and dashed toward the truck.

When we'd gotten out of the way, we both turned around and watched the helicopter slowly lift off.

I could still feel the excitement running through her as she glanced over at me.

"Do you this for all the ladies?" she asked.

"First time." I smiled, staring straight at the chopper.

"Really? I find that hard to believe."

I laughed and brought my gaze to hers. "Believe it or not, Lana..."

"What?" she whispered, stepping closer.

"I've never done any of the things we've done together with another woman."

Her smile only widened as she stepped closer, and I looped my arms around her waist.

"You're the first person I've ever been able to open up to and relax around without worrying about what you'll think."

"I like that answer," she said softly, her voice turning breathy.

My gaze stayed on Lana's as she pressed her body into mine. Everything about her surrounded me in music. Her words turned to lyrics. Her heartbeat created a new tempo. She was opening doors that I'd firmly decided to close, but I knew that opening them back up brought its own issues.

Starting a relationship with someone who's

spending a year in the studio making music and then a year on the road promoting isn't conducive to anything more than letting people housesit your home, as I seemed to become a pro at.

"You going to kiss me or what?" she teased, standing on her toes.

Without waiting a second more, I held her close and brought my mouth to hers. She let out a wistful sigh and moan as her hands ran slowly along my sides. The flick and swirl of her tongue reminded me of how much more I wanted from her.

Lana's lips broke from mine, and she flashed a sloppy grin. "You're kind of addicting."

"I could say the same, Lana. It's hard to get you out of my mind."

She lit up at those words, but they were true. "What are we going to do after all this?"

I drew a deep breath and glanced toward the wide-open sky. "I don't know, but it's not going to be easy."

She touched her finger to my lips. "No, it's not."

"Things feel so easy when I'm with you."

Lana nodded. "I know. I keep telling myself it's because I'm on vacation."

"That started with a funeral," I added.

Lana smirked and folded her arms over her chest. "Well, maybe a girl can only go up from there."

I chuckled. "That's always been my motto. Start the bar really low, and then you'll be pleasantly surprised since you can only go up."

"I almost believe that coming from you, but I looked up how many Grammys you have."

For the first time in a long time, I didn't feel awkward or like I was being used. I just felt proud.

"Yeah? And what did you think?"

"Kind of impressive, if you're impressed by those sorts of things."

"Are you?" I asked, smiling.

"Not really. No." She shook her head. "But I think it's pretty cool that you've found your calling."

"But you know it's still work, right?"

She rolled her eyes. "Fancy hotels, big parties, lots of praise, even more money." She chuckled. "Sounds rough."

"When you put it that way..." I watched Lana and nodded. "I'm sure I'll sound ridiculous saying it, but it's not quite like that. My life is more about being alone on a tour bus, hearing about sensational parties I wouldn't want to go to anyway, and wondering what life is really about."

Lana laughed. "I think you spend too much time thinking."

That was a first. "Really?"

She clasped her fingers around mine. "I don't doubt you have a lonely life, but I think you've probably touched more lives than you could ever imagine. Music is an important part of people's lives. It helps us get through the happy times, the sad times, and the in-between times."

I smiled and nodded. "So you're a fan of music. Just not mine."

Lana blushed and grinned. "I like your music the most when I want to be sad. It just so happens that I don't like being sad."

"I have a confession, Lana."

"What's that?"

"It's going to be really hard when you go back to Washington." I grinned. "You keep me off-balance just enough to make life interesting."

"Good."

Even though there hadn't been a mention of rain for days, a few clouds started coating the brilliant blue sky.

"You hungry?" I asked.

"Starving."

The first raindrop hit, and we hurried to the truck.

By the time we'd made it to town, the sprinkles had turned to a downpour, but it didn't spoil our conversation any. We'd covered her dad living in Arizona and rarely visiting, and my parents, who I'd managed not to see as regularly as I'd hoped without going into why.

I pulled into the parking lot of the restaurant I'd made reservations at and glanced at Lana, who was quietly looking out the window. I wondered what she was thinking about. Had I said too much? Made it sound like I wasn't grateful? Because I was more grateful than most. Or was she thinking about the reason she was brought to Montana in the first place?

"It's a beautiful little place," she said, eyeing the restaurant.

The rustic building was on the lake, with patios surrounding the entire backside. Pots with overflowing white geraniums and explosions of hot pink impatiens dotted the walkway leading to the door.

"I hope you're hungry. I haven't had a chance to eat at that many places since I've moved here, but this is a favorite," I told her as we made our way to the front of the truck.

I slipped my hand over hers, and we walked toward the restaurant.

"I still can't believe I saw Montana from a helicopter." She smiled. "A chartered helicopter."

"I hope you liked it."

"I'm still in shock, to be honest." She smiled as I opened the door, and we stepped inside. "It's like from the moment I've met you, my life has become something made of dreams."

I wanted to freeze this moment. We were running out of time. There wasn't any way to make her fall in love with me in nine days. That was ridiculous and something right out of a country song. In fact, that was how country songs were made. A whirlwind romance was a recipe for disaster.

But it didn't feel like a whirlwind with Lana. It felt easy and comfortable and like we'd known one another forever. It was an odd sensation.

As I walked up to the hostess, her eyes widened, her cheeks turned scarlet, and she lost all ability to speak.

"Two for dinner reservations under Jacob Miller."

The hostess continued to stare and nodded, grabbing two menus. I glanced at Lana, who seemed to be getting a kick out of the spectacle. The hostess tripped, which just made me feel bad. I helped her regain her footing, and that was when she'd gotten her voice back.

"Mr. Miller, I hate to ask." She glanced at me. "But can I get your autograph?"

I looked at Lana, who nodded.

"Of course."

"Thank you. My mom is absolutely in love with your music." She grabbed a napkin and pen. "She'll never believe I ran into you. I know all of your songs. I grew up having to listen to them. They're always so sad, but it fits perfectly because my mom got divorced from my dad, so there's that."

Lana snickered as I quickly asked for the name of the hostess's mom.

As soon as we sat down, Lana leaned over and giggled. "Her mom, huh?"

"I wondered how long it would take before you picked up on that."

Lana grinned and raised the menu. "Oh, I picked up on that right away."

I chuckled and shook my head as I stared at a menu. "I can't tell you what a relief it is not to have someone kiss my ass all the time."

She lowered her menu. "Well, I'm sure you have a lovely one, but I have yet been offered a chance to see it."

I flashed a wicked grin and felt electricity zip

between us as our eyes stayed on one another.

"You know, it's not the first time that's happened recently."

Lana's eyes widened. "Someone has asked to see your ass?"

I cracked up and shook my head. "No, having to do autographs for parents."

"Ah, the age-old problem with rock stars. They get old." Her green eyes twinkled with mischief, and I felt like the luckiest man in the world. I never knew what was going to come out of Lana's mouth, but what I did know was that she had the most beautiful smile I'd ever seen.

"Will you spend tomorrow with me?" I asked.

She winked at me. "I was counting on it."

And Lana Roberts made me the happiest man on the planet.

CHAPTER FIFTEEN

Lana

My sister's grinning face was on my phone as I got ready for the day.

"Are you sure you're going to come back to Cloudberry?" Samantha teased.

I dabbed on some mascara in the mirror and then picked up my phone to talk to my sister.

"Jacob just happens to be a very good tour guide."

My sister laughed. "Of a town he's barely lived in."

I grinned. "You'd be surprised."

"I still can't believe he planned a helicopter ride for you."

Just the memory warmed me up inside, and I let out a happy sigh. "It was pretty incredible."

"I can imagine," Samantha said wryly.

"Actually, everything he's come up with has been special." I grinned and looked into the phone. "It's exactly what I needed."

"You've needed to get away for eons," Samantha said, smiling. "I just never expected that you'd run away with a country star, but you've always been full of surprises."

Just the mere thought of Jacob Miller made me grin like a dummy. What I loved the most was that the smiles in recent days had all been real, genuine smiles. They weren't the smiles I'd learned to plaster on my face whenever things weren't going how'd I'd hoped.

"If you want to extend your trip, you know we have you covered."

My chest tightened at the thought. I liked the idea that I was only here for a short time. It was almost like if I stayed a day past what I'd planned, my pumpkin carriage would explode and my glass slipper would shatter.

I knew nothing was perfect. I learned that the hard way with finding out about my parents' relationship, but I wanted to leave Montana with the same feeling I had now—pure bliss.

"I'd better get going. He's meeting me in the lobby. We're headed to the farmers' market and then headed back to his place."

"Oh," Samantha cooed. "That sounds promising."

I chuckled and rolled my eyes. "Not gonna happen. He's the best kisser in the world, but I don't think my heart could handle a one-night stand with him."

"Why not just *not* make plans?" Samantha suggested. "Just let life go where it's meant to go."

"No wonder all of your books sneak in a love story," I grumbled.

"I'm just saying you don't have to plan everything in life."

"Have a nice day, Sam. Love ya." I clicked the red *x* on my phone before she could put any other bad ideas in my head.

The truth was that every time we'd kissed, my mind went directly to the next step with Jacob. I wanted to see what was under his clothes, feel his skin against mine and his lips everywhere they hadn't been.

But everything had been absolutely perfect with Jacob, and I didn't want to ruin anything.

I slipped my phone in my small purse, grabbed a white sweater to pull over my pink dress, and headed out the door. The moment I made it to the lobby, I saw a group of women surrounding some poor soul. As I made my way over to the man at the center of all, he looked absolutely relieved as he signed a few more scraps of paper before everyone disbanded.

"Did you have your manager organize this or something just so I knew you were extra famous?"

Jacob kissed the top of my head, and an overwhelming amount of comfort spread through me. A simple gesture like that shouldn't make me feel like we'd be together long after this trip, but it did. Those hopes and dreams started skidding through me at an unstoppable pace.

I glanced at Jacob, who was studying me closely.

"What are you thinking?" he asked.

"It's long and complicated and messy and ridiculous."

He rubbed his hands together and grinned. "Sounds like my kind of topic."

"Believe me, you'll think I'm crazy."

"Try me." He eyed me, resting his arm over my shoulders and pulling me in for another kiss on the top of my head. "By the way, you look beautiful."

"And practical." I smiled, glancing at my white sneakers I'd paired with my dress.

"Yes, and practical." He laughed as we started outside. "So, tell me what you were thinking a second ago."

I drew a deep breath and kept my gaze forward. "I was thinking how nice it is with you and how I don't want this to end, but I know it has to end because you are a country star, and I'm an innkeeper. You live in Montana, and I live in Washington. This is just a vacation fling. But I loved how that kiss made me feel."

He slowed and turned to face me, tipping my chin

up slightly. "Why does this have to end?"

I shifted my weight from one foot to the other and squinted as the bright sun skewed my vision.

"I just gave you my list."

Jacob shook his head. "No, you gave me logistics."

"Huh?"

"Reasons this thing between us has to end would be something like..." He bit his lip, and I suddenly wanted to bite it too. "Let's see, a good reason would be if you didn't like me. If you didn't like me kissing you. If you didn't like spending time with me. Those are reasons to end something, not because we don't live in convenient locations or have convenient jobs."

"But it's not very practical."

"Why does love have to be practical?" Jacob asked.

I shielded my eyes from the sun so Jacob could come back into focus. "I guess it doesn't."

"Tell me the real reason you want this to end." He flicked his fingers and smiled. "Let me have it."

"Because I'm scared that I'll get my heart broken." I swallowed down another lump that sprang from nowhere thanks to this Montana air, but it was true.

I thought back to my mom and the secret she kept from us all to protect us, to let us believe in a certain kind of love. She knew our dad wasn't faithful, but she didn't say a word. She loved my dad in front of us and away from us. She took care of him as a woman who loved a man does. Was it right? Maybe not. But that was my mom's choice. Or maybe it was my mom's revenge.

She loved him so hard that he couldn't go a day without thinking about what he had done to my mom.

But now that I knew about Charlotte and her mom, it became impossible not to feel bad for her as well.

Jacob didn't say anything. Instead, he waited for me to say more.

"I don't want to have what happened to my mom to happen to me or what happened to poor Charlotte's mom." I shook my head. "I just... it's hard to believe my dad would do that to two women and not think twice."

Jacob rubbed my arms softly before pulling me in.

"Lana, something tells me your dad thinks of what he's done every single day. I wouldn't be surprised if that's why he's hidden away from all of you."

"He doesn't even know about Charlotte," I said softly. "Or that we know."

"But he knows what he did. He can't hide his own truth from himself. Secret daughter or not, he knows what he did to his wife."

I looked into Jacob's eyes and nodded. "And my mom loved him to the very end."

"That's the love you want to treasure, Lana. That's pure." He slid his hand over mine, and I felt a pull to him that I couldn't ignore.

"But I don't want to be the one giving all the love and not getting it in return," I said, unable to understand how Jacob could pull so much from me. I dabbed some dampness from my eyes and cleared my throat.

"I wouldn't want that either."

"Okay. It's suddenly gotten way too serious for a Montana vacation. Let's go to that farmers' market before they sell out of dinner."

He wouldn't let me walk away. Instead, he pulled me closer. "Lana, promise me you'll work on one thing while we're together."

"What's that?"

"Trust. Trust that not all men cheat." Jacob smiled sheepishly. "I'm sure that coming from a musician on the road is rich, but it's true. Not all men are heartless."

I nodded slowly and smiled. "Okay, Cowboy. I'll work on that."

By the time we got to the farmers' market, it was as if the heavy conversations had happened many moons ago, and the most serious topic at hand was what kind of vegetable to grill with the steaks he had marinating at his house.

As far as the eye could see, tiny white tent tops dotted the market with crowds clutching bouquets of flowers, bags of green beans, and fresh honey sticks.

I spotted a vendor with local soaps. "We've got to go over there."

"Fine by me."

I tugged on Jacob's hand, and he quickly pivoted

to make his way toward the soap store.

So many fragrances hit my senses as we stepped into the booth. In one direction lemon wafted over to me, and when I turned my head, a lovely rose scent drifted over.

"I'm in heaven," I whispered.

"I've been in heaven."

"You're too smooth, buckaroo," I teased, reaching for a pink and gold wrapped soap. I brought it to my nose and sniffed, closing my eyes. "Incredible."

I stuck it up to his nose, and he sniffed and then sneezed.

"Looks like you might be allergic to me for the next couple of weeks." I grinned, grabbing an orange spice soap next. The sweet and spicy smell made me extremely happy, along with a peppermint soap I spotted.

"Don't I get to smell them anymore?" he asked, coming up behind me as I placed the soaps on the counter where a man was sitting with his book.

"No. You lost that opportunity when you sneezed on them."

Jacob chuckled and rubbed my shoulders as the man rang up my purchase. Before I had a chance to pay, Jacob had already slid the man his credit card.

I spun around and shook my head. "You didn't have to do that."

"It's the least I could do since I sneezed on your favorite soap."

I smiled and turned back to the man and thanked him for making such lovely soaps as I took the bag from him.

"Now, it's my turn," Jacob said, pointing toward a booth with various bird houses lined up.

"Really?" I looked up at Jacob, who looked like a kid in a candy store as we got closer.

He shrugged and grinned. "Yeah. So what?"

I chuckled. "I didn't know you were a birder."

"Call me what you want, but who doesn't like seeing birds in their yard?" He reached for a tiny yellow house with bright red trim and a pinwheel on top.

"I'm impressed," I whispered. "You're not looking to blend in with your bird houses."

"Go big or go home." He bent over and checked out another that looked like a gothic mansion.

"Did you have bird houses at your San Fran house?"

"No, but I need a hobby. I'm retired, remember?"

"Ah, at the ripe old age of thirty—wait, thirty... what was it again?"

Jacob smiled as he pulled the two birdhouses off the shelves and went over and paid for them.

I noticed a group of ladies huddling near the booth and hid a smile. I was pretty sure they were looking for an autograph.

The moment he turned around, the women all jumped up and waved as he walked over to me and slid his arm around my waist.

It wasn't until we walked into the aisle that he realized a group of women were eagerly awaiting his arrival.

"I'm so sorry," one of the women asked, glancing at me. "Do you mind if we get a picture?"

Jacob looked at me as if to apologize, but I got a complete kick out of it as he got swarmed by a small army of women. They all took turns with their phones, and when they'd all gotten their turn, he walked over to me.

"Let's grab some veggies and book."

"For a famous guy, you don't seem to be drawn to fame."

"I'm grateful for the perks it's given my family, but I could care less." He smiled.

"Except when it slowly starts dawning on you that it's the moms of all the teenagers who want your autographs," I teased. "That's got to be almost as tough as being called Ma'am by a sexy superstar."

We reached the vegetable stand at the end of the aisle, and I pointed at some corn and green beans. "How about those?"

"Looks perfect."

I quickly bagged a couple of ears of corn and shoveled in some green beans and set them on the counter to pay. I slid some cash on the counter and completed the transaction before Jacob had a chance to be sneaky.

"You ready?" I asked. "I'm starving."

The wind started picking up, and he slowly moved a piece of stray hair from my face. The gentle touch did incredible things to me. I was in rough shape. I didn't know how I'd survive the night being locked up alone in a beautiful home all evening with Jacob.

CHAPTER SIXTEEN

Jacob

Seeing Lana in an innocent pink dress and a pair of white sneakers drew my mind to some dirty places. There was something so absolutely effortless about her sexiness, and I was pretty sure that she didn't even know what she could do to me.

We'd made it back to my place, and all I could think about was how amazing it would be if I could lather the soap that she'd just bought all over her naked body.

We were in the kitchen. She was across the island from me, but all I could think about was kissing her bare skin from head to toe.

I could usually keep my act together, but there was something that just pulled to me. It didn't matter if it was one of her cute little grins or the way she'd teased me endlessly about my ego.

I just loved spending time with her, and soon, she'd be gone.

Just as Lana enjoyed pointing out, she'd be back in Washington running her inn, and I'd be in Montana bemoaning my fate.

"You've suddenly gotten quiet," Lana said, looking up from cutting her pile of green beans. "It worries me."

I smiled. "I think it's finally hit me that you're leaving Montana in a week."

She tapped her finger on the counter and nodded. "It's coming up quickly."

"It is. I've really liked having you around."

"Me too." She tucked her hair behind her ears and went back to chopping the green bean ends. "You think you might come out to Washington for a visit?"

"It's definitely moved up on my list of things to

do."

She brought her soft green eyes to me and smiled. "Yeah?"

I nodded.

"I'd like that."

"Will you hear me out about something?" I asked.

She let out a low whistle and nodded. "Sounds serious."

I chuckled, turning up Kenny Rogers and Dolly Parton's duet, *Islands in the Stream*. "Not too serious."

She looked around the kitchen to see where the music came from. "All right. Let me have it."

Was this one of the corniest moves of all time? Probably, but I couldn't help it. Lana made me remember what it was like to be full of joy. The last person to do that was my sister when we were just kids.

"Okay." I inhaled a breath and wondered how to approach it. "Will you do me the honor of singing once with me?"

She scowled and looked around the kitchen. "What do you mean? Here? To this song? I mean, I love

Kenny and Dolly, but..."

I laughed. "I guess we could sing here, but I was thinking on a karaoke night back at the lodge."

"Why?" Her scowl deepened.

"I..." Sliding my phone over to her, I drew another breath. "I wrote a duet, and I'd love if you'd sing it with me."

"Umm. I've never done that before." She looked down at the screen and read the first line and then continued aloud to the very end.

I want an impractical love
You want a wishing well

But don't tell me it can't be
I'll dig that well if you give me that love

Oh, but it's complicated what you do.

Tell me how I got into this need
This need of impractical love

I need you, and you need me
Our old world can burn down

Down in that well
Do what you want

Just do it with me
I'll do it with you.

Oh, but it's complicated what you do

I have that wishing well
You have my heart

But will you run around
Will I fade away

But it's impractical love
I found what I wasn't even looking for

Don't mind the distance
I won't mind that wishing well

Oh, but it's complicated what we do.

With our impractical love

Lana slowly rose her head, and her eyes filled with tears as she nodded. "This is incredible."

"Is that a yes?" I asked. "Or no? You're hard to read."

She swallowed and wiped away the tears. "It's a yes, but I don't want to screw it up."

"You'll make it perfect." I smiled and made my way over to Lana. "You are perfect."

"How can you still be single?" Her eyes stayed on mine.

I laughed. "I could say the same about you."

She chuckled and playfully knocked my chin. "Then why don't you?"

"I just did."

She laughed harder, and I spun her around, trying to memorize every single part of this moment with Lana.

"You know what's crazy?" she asked as I set her

back on the ground.

"That I got you to say yes to singing one more time in front of people?" I waggled my brows.

"No. That you actually wrote a happy song. I mean, it's still very layered, but it's happy."

"Yeah?"

She smiled and nodded. "Yeah. For starters, I didn't wind up in the well. No horse trotted over me. No ex-wife showed up. I mean, it's a pretty peppy song for you."

"What can I say? You bring it out in me."

"Good." Her eyes dropped to my lips. "What would you say if we worked up a bit of an appetite before we put the steaks on the grill?"

Her words surprised me yet again. This woman would always keep me on my toes.

I nodded and grinned. "Well, I'd say that's one of the best ideas I've ever heard."

She bit her bottom lip and her gaze met mine.

The heat rolling through me was nearly unbearable, and before I knew it, she'd jumped into my arms, wrapping her legs around my waist.

"There are some perks to looking like a beanstalk," she teased, and I shook my head.

"Stop it, Lana. You're the most beautiful woman I've ever laid eyes on. You're perfect."

She cocked her head, looking surprised. "Really?"

"Really."

"Take me to the bedroom, Jacob, or I'll never talk to you again."

The heat between us was explosive. "But this might be the most impractical love in the world," I teased.

She winked at me. "I don't care."

By the time I carried her to the bedroom, my lips were on hers, and she was slowly moving her hips through our clothes.

I placed her on my bed and smiled, taking in how beautiful this moment was and how I never wanted it to end.

I smiled and shook my head as she pulled her clothes off.

"I want to nibble every part of you."

She chuckled. "Like Jaqueline and the carrots?"

"No, more like this." My mouth moved along her belly, and rather than nibbling of any sort, my tongue slid along her bare skin.

She wiggled underneath me, and it was the best feeling ever as my fingers moved between her legs.

I brought Lana to the brink and then backed off, teasing all of her senses with the pause of time and kisses between us.

My hands ran along her sides as my mouth explored a damp trail, the hum of my voice vibrating a fiery need through us as my tongue tasted her sweetness, leading her so close but knowing exactly when to stop.

A pouty mewl left her lips as she fisted my shirt through her fingers.

"No more teasing," she whispered as her eyes locked on mine.

"Yeah?"

She smiled sweetly. "You heard me."

I pulled my shirt over my head, and her hands skated down my abs. To say I was in awe would be putting it lightly. Just the mere touch from her fingers put me dangerously close to the edge.

I'd done plenty of imagining since I'd met her, but I didn't realize that simply her touch would do so much.

"You must have a lot of time on your hands to look this good." She looped her arms over my neck.

Our eyes met again, and I smiled.

"More than I care to admit."

Her hands fell to the buttons of my jeans and quickly worked to unfasten them. I crawled off the bed and climbed out of the rest of my clothing, but all I could focus on was how gorgeous her naked body was in my bed. I climbed over Lana and caged her in with my arms as I kissed her neck, moving to her collarbone and down to her left breast and then her right.

A little moan escaped her lips, and I thought I'd made my way to heaven and back. Her fingernails gently scraped against my back, and she looped her legs around my waist as she teased me endlessly until I entered her.

She let out a moan to match mine as I felt inside

her, felt like we were one. Our worlds built on one another as pleasure ripped through us and our breathing turned ragged, and she held me so tightly in her arms as our bodies succumbed to the onslaught of sensations pulsing through us both.

And when I thought it couldn't get any better, Lana turned over and snuggled into me. "You know, that felt like a very practical love, if you ask me."

Her words made me a very happy man as I nuzzled into her neck and wrapped my arms over her slender waist.

CHAPTER SEVENTEEN

Lana

I stared at Jacob. "Okay, I can't blame any pink squirrel for saying yes to you about this whole singing the duet, but I can fully blame you for everything you did to me to put me in this situation." I pretended to stomp my foot, and Jacob only laughed. "Seriously. I was under major duress the other night. I was in need."

Jacob chuckled. "Just like the song talks about."

I rolled my eyes and smiled. "You're gonna be hard to leave, Cowboy."

And it was true. That night was the most special

night of my entire life. The way he looked at me as he made love to me. The way his breathing changed when I took control and when he took control back. The way our bodies melded together. The way he held me.

"You're looking pretty happy," Jacob said, waving the bartender over.

I smiled. "Just reminiscing."

Jacob's brows shot up with a mischievous spark behind his gaze. "Yeah? What about?"

I laughed and shook my head. "You're awful, getting me all worked up like this right before I'm about to go on stage to sing a song I barely know in front of complete strangers."

Grey walked over and grinned. "Hey, stranger. I thought I'd see you back in here long ago."

I grinned and blushed. "It's been a busy week."

"I guess." Grey glanced at the stage. "Gonna get back up there?"

I nodded and wagged my finger. "But no pink squirrels for me tonight."

"Whatever you say." Grey nodded and looked at

Jacob. "Can I get you anything?"

"I'll take a Jack and Coke."

"Got it." Grey smiled and glanced at me. "Anything? How about a club soda?"

"That sounds perfect." I nodded and watched Grey walk away. "You know, it's so crazy how many interesting people I've met since I left the inn. Don't get me wrong, we have a ton of fascinating guests, but there's something about being out in the world."

Jacob nodded. "I think it's just you, Lana. I think you bring out the best in people."

I grinned, and a wave of nerves washed through me as Grey brought our drinks.

"Okay. I change my mind," I confessed, leaning toward Grey. "I think I need something. Maybe a beer."

"Sure thing. Any one in particular?" he asked, glancing at the chalkboard with a list of the latest microbrews. I narrowed my eyes as the names came into focus. "How about the IPA?"

"Good choice."

"Thanks." I cozied into my seat just as the lights went down. "Oh, no."

Jacob glanced around. "What?"

"Karaoke is starting." I shook my head, feeling my palms get moist. "I'm not ready."

"You can back out if you want," Jacob challenged.

I flashed him a dirty look. "I'm not a quitter."

"Of course not." Jacob's smile curled into a smirk.

Grey brought over my IPA, and the first guy got onto the stage.

Jacob looked around again.

"You waiting for someone?" I asked.

Jacob shrugged. "My manager mentioned that he might be in town, but I don't see him."

"Hmph." I took a sip of the IPA and listened to the first singer.

By the third singer and second IPA, the fear had turned to exhilaration. My fingers even tingled when I thought about gripping the microphone.

I leaned into the table. "You ready, Cowboy?"

Surprise dotted his expression. "Are you?"

I nodded, smiling. "I am."

"Nice." He had a tiny jump drive in his hand.

"What's that?" I asked.

241

"The background music for our song."

"What? How?"

"I have connections," he teased.

I laughed, realizing how ridiculous it was to be surprised that the man with a million Billboard hits could get someone to record a track for him.

"You're taking this pretty seriously," I said, eyeing the little device.

"I don't know when I'll get this opportunity with you again."

Jacob's words stung hard. I'd been trying to bury the fact that I'd be leaving in a few days, but it was true. When would we ever get this opportunity again?

I nodded as he stood and walked over to the bartender in charge of the playlist. I watched Jacob explain everything to him and saw the bartender get really animated.

By the time Jacob came back to the table, I was ready for another IPA, but I knew better. As of now, I could remember the lyrics. Another IPA from now, it would be iffy.

I had to fight through the fear that suddenly

replaced the exhilaration I was reveling in only minutes ago.

As a woman finished up a Taylor Swift song, Jacob reached for my hand.

"You're going to knock them dead."

"Well, I hope not." I grimaced. "I've already been to one funeral this week."

He squeezed my hand and laughed. "Man, you're awesome."

"Or just different."

"Different is fine by me," he whispered next to my ear, which sent a thrill of shivers through me.

As the crowd cheered our wannabe Taylor Swift, we stepped to the side so she could walk down the stairs.

My hands started trembling as I thought about what I was about to do.

"Just follow my lead." He kept hold of my hand, which was probably no longer just clammy but drenched as we walked onto the stage.

The bartender magically appeared with two chairs, sheet music, and the words also on the karaoke screen.

Jacob had this planned far beyond what I'd imagined.

I scanned the audience and was grateful the blinding lights made it difficult to see much in the way of features.

As the soft, somewhat upbeat melody played, I was in shock.

The music sounded real, like this had already been played on radios and streamed online.

I looked over at Jacob, who was tapping his knee, and then it was time.

Before I started drowning in worry, I began to sing. My voice matched Jacob's, the words fell from my lips, and I wanted nothing more than to sing Jacob's song a million times over.

I saw the crowd swaying, clapping, and nodding.

It felt like a dream. The kind that is packaged up so tidily when you're six and in your bathroom singing in front of a mirror with a hairbrush.

Jacob's hand rested on my knee as we finished the last line, and I felt like the world was mine for the taking.

Because of the man next to me.

The crowd started cheering, and once they quieted down, the bartender grabbed a microphone as we started off the stage.

"Ladies and gentlemen, I've just been informed that we here in Big Fork, Montana just heard what's going to be Jacob Miller's new single called *Impractical Love.*"

I turned to look at Jacob.

"I hope you'll record it with me sometime."

My mouth fell open as he held my hand. I moved toward the steps, and out of nowhere, Lars appeared in the audience.

Terror shot through me.

My ankle twisted, and I nearly fell to the ground when Jacob caught me from behind.

I quickly scanned where I thought I had seen him and swallowed down my embarrassment.

My system was on complete overload.

"Are you okay?" Jacob whispered. "I'm so sorry. I guess that wasn't the best spot to ask that."

I shook my head and smiled briefly before wincing from the pain in my ankle. "No, it wasn't you or what you said."

As the crowd died down, the next act went up.

I tried to walk on my ankle, but a shooting pain darted through my foot and leg simultaneously.

"Let me carry you."

I shook my head, trying to spot Lars.

"Who are you looking for?" Jacob asked.

I spun awkwardly on one foot. "I think I just saw Lars."

Jacob smiled until he saw that I was serious. "Where?"

I pointed toward the back of the bar and squinted when I saw him again. "That guy. Right there."

The man saw me pointing and started coming toward us. My heart started pounding in my chest. It wasn't that I didn't believe in ghosts. I mean, we might almost have had a couple at the inn. There had been a lot of unexplained happenings there, and my mom was certain we had them.

But this...

This didn't make a lick of sense.

I curled my hands around Jacob's arm as the man got feet away from us, and I quickly realized that up close, this man wasn't Lars, but he was strange.

"Hey," he said, smiling at Jacob and glancing at me. "Sorry I'm late. I got in just in time to see you two."

Jacob nodded and grinned. "She's great, isn't she?"

"Like an angel. You have a hit."

That was when I realized it was Jacob's manager.

"You were right. You just needed time away. Granted, it's only been a couple of weeks, but you've always worked at the speed of light."

His manager rubbed me the wrong way, but the pain in my ankle was only getting worse.

So much so that I decided it was time for me to make an exit to my room and order a big bag of ice and let these two rehash the good old days of three weeks ago or whatever it's been.

"Hey, Jacob," I said softly, feeling the burning turning to throbbing.

His eyes fell to mine.

"I think I'm going to head back to my room. I really twisted my ankle."

"Let me come with you. I can carry you."

I shook my head, suddenly feeling like everything wasn't necessarily about us but maybe just Jacob's song.

"I'm fine, really. Catch up, and I'll see you tomorrow. Promise." I lifted my bad foot and balanced on my good one as I pecked his cheek.

He caught my hand in his, and I knew he wanted me to stay, but I could only fake it for so long.

At this rate, I'd probably be crawling to my room.

Jacob kissed me one last time, and I said a quick bye to the man I didn't even bother getting a name for as I hobbled over to Grey.

"You were phenomenal."

"Thanks," I said, suddenly feeling shy. "Jacob just wrote that."

"He's talented."

I nodded and leaned over the bar. "I know this is a weird request, but can you have someone send a bag or two of ice? I twisted my ankle, and it's killing me."

"Sure. No problem."

I glanced toward Jacob and saw his gaze on me as I did my best to look like I was walking normally. His manager came all the way to Montana. I wasn't about to act like the damsel in distress.

I'd been clumsy enough in life to know how to take care of my battered self.

But as I made my way to the hotel room, the pain was excruciating.

By the time I got inside and flopped on the bed, I knew I was in trouble. This wasn't a sprain. What also bothered me was the fact that Jacob knew his manager was going to be here to listen to us sing together. It didn't really click when he'd mentioned that his manager might be in town. It sounded more casual, not that his manager was coming to listen to us. That didn't sit well with me. Jacob had been after me this entire time to sing again. What if that was all he was after, finding talent for his manager?

No, I was just grumpy because my foot felt like it was in the process of falling off.

A knock sounded at the door, and I somehow

managed enough oomph to roll off the bed and hop over to the door, ready for that bag of ice.

When I swung open the door, Jacob was standing at the door with a bag of ice and a plate full of carrots.

CHAPTER EIGHTEEN

Jacob

This wasn't how I saw Lana's vacation ending. We had another week left, give or take, and I was determined to convince her to stay even longer.

Instead, I wound up driving her to the hospital last night, where they diagnosed her with multiple fractures. She was at my house with her leg in a cast propped up on several pillows. This morning around three o'clock, I thought about the silver lining of this whole ordeal. We'd get to know one another really well while I took care of her.

But that idea sailed right out the window this

morning when I found out her sister was flying out here today to drive Lana home.

It was like these last several days had never existed.

Except that I knew in my heart that they did, and our time together mattered.

Seeing Lana on the pain medicine, however, made me wonder if she'd remember much of anything by the time her leg healed.

"Cowboy," Lana's voice rang through my house, and I treasured the sound. "Where's my cowboy?"

I smiled and made my way to the bedroom with a fresh cup of coffee and a croissant on a tray.

"For me?" Her eyes sparkled. "How did you get a croissant here? Please tell me you're not also a baker."

I laughed and shook my head. "Grey dropped off a bag of pastries from where his girlfriend works."

Lana snickered. "Maybe I should be dating her."

"If it made you stay in town, I'd be game."

"Are you really going to miss me, Cowboy?" Her eyes looked happy, but edged with a bit more of a dopy Lana mixed pain from her ankle.

"More than you'll ever know."

"Try me. I love details." She patted the bed, and I laughed as I sat next to her.

Pillows surrounded Lana, and she looked like a princess in a castle of fluff.

I smiled. "Fine. I'll tell you everything that's going through my mind."

"That might not take *too* long." She chuckled, and all it did was make me want to wrestle her into my arms and make love to her again, but I couldn't. "Seriously, I have a long drive back to Washington, and I'd love to daydream about my little fairy-tale vacation." She took a bite of the croissant and moaned. "I might not be kidding about dating Grey's girlfriend."

I laughed, unsure of how much Lana would actually remember from this conversation.

"Being with you made me realize what I've been missing in life. I had a hunch, but I wasn't sure." I rested my hand on her good leg. "When I'd left San Francisco, I'd given up on not just music, but what my life had become."

"That's not good." She shook her head.

I laughed. "No, it's not."

"Well, I have a secret too."

"Yeah?" I asked, unsure of which way this conversation might suddenly turn. I glanced out the window at the lake, wishing we could go on it just one more time.

"I…"

She stopped, and I whipped my head back to see her completely zonked, croissant in hand, coffee still on the tray, mouth open just a little, eyes closed.

I chuckled and shook my head. "Damn. I have a feeling you were about to say something good too." I slowly pulled the croissant from her hands, and her fingers did a death grip on the pastry, so I let go. She could cuddle with it as long as she needed, but I did grab the cup of coffee off the tray and set it on the nightstand.

Lana started snoring softly, and I smiled, knowing just how much I would miss this woman.

Part of me worried that Lana would be upset when I showed up in her hotel room last night. I didn't like how Ted treated the whole situation. It made things just feel creepy and planned, which it hadn't been.

I thought back to my sister, and my chest tightened. I rarely let myself think about everything that led to her death. It was like if I didn't think about it, it didn't happen.

But I knew it had, and her death blew my family's world apart.

The loss drove me to depths of despair I didn't know were possible.

All things I knew I could share with Lana or could have shared with Lana until everything blew up last night.

I shook my head and made my way to the kitchen. Things had been going so well, and then she thought she saw a dead guy who happened to be my manager.

If she hadn't broken her ankle, it would have been kind of funny, especially since Ted was so Hollywood. He'd already had his eyes done by the time he'd hit forty, and that was twenty years ago. But I could actually see the resemblance between Ted and Lars.

They both liked to dress edgy, but in Ted's case, it didn't quite work.

When I reached for my phone and poured myself a cup of coffee, I saw a couple of texts from Ted.

Do you think you could convince her to lay down that track with you?

This could be exactly what you need to get your head back in the game.

Call me. Text me. Tell me something.

I shook my head. "Right, Ted. The woman just broke her ankle, and you want me to sit down and make some firm plans for my music career." I spun my phone away. "Not happening."

As if that response put a call out to lurking managers, my doorbell rang. I didn't even have to look out the window to know it was Ted.

I opened the door and leaned on it while I sipped my coffee.

"What's up?"

"Why haven't you responded?" Ted looked impatient and restless.

"I'm playing nurse right now." I shook my head and took another sip. "What's gotten into you?"

"That girl's voice is breathtaking, and together you two are—"

"She's all woman, Ted. She's also laid up in bed with multiple fractures, pain medicine, and a sister flying out here to drive her back to Washington. When, precisely, would you like me to ask her about a duet? Before or after she's dozing off from all the meds she's on?"

"Listen, I recorded a snippet, not more than a few seconds, but the record company is all over it." He glanced inside. "You know you owe them another record."

I smiled and nodded. "I know, but there's no time limit to get the record out."

"You're enough to make me quit the business," Ted grumbled.

"You know you'd miss it and me." I winked at him,

which I knew only pissed him off more.

"Listen, Ted. I'm excited to see what the future holds, but now is not the time to bother Lana with any of it. The song can wait. Why'd you come here, anyway?"

"To see if I could gauge whether you were giving it all up." His pointy brows arched up. "And I was relieved to see that you love music as much as you always have."

I shrugged, knowing it was Lana, not the music, that made the fire in me roar back to life.

"If you let her get away, mark my words. Someone else will snatch her up."

"Ted, she doesn't want to be found. It's not like she's posting clips of herself singing on social media. If it's meant to be, it will be."

"This Montana air has gotten to you." Ted smiled. "Just promise me that you'll bring it up to her."

"I will." I let out a sigh. "I just can't promise when."

"When will her leg be fixed?" Ted asked.

"Fixed? Well, it could take eight weeks for it to heal, and then she has to go through physical therapy."

"Just don't let her get away."

"I don't think she'll be hobbling anywhere, Ted, but I'm sure she'll be flattered that you cared."

His eyes turned beady, and I knew he was dreaming of another hit under his belt and bank account. I swore I could see a faint outline of a dollar sign in his pupils.

"Listen, I should get Lana ready for when her sister arrives."

"No inviting me in for coffee?" he asked, glancing behind me.

"Tomorrow."

I knew better than to let him get his talons into Lana while she's medicated.

"Fine. I'll see you tomorrow."

I nodded. "Let's meet at the lodge for breakfast at ten o'clock."

"All right." He gave a wave as he spun around and made his way to his rental car. How he found a Porsche to rent in Montana was beyond me, but it took some extra effort.

I closed the door and went to the kitchen to pour

myself more coffee when *Take on Me* by a-ha faintly drifted down the hallway, and I chuckled.

"She must be up," I said to myself, loving the thought as I made my way down the hall.

The closer I got to the bedroom, the louder the synthesizer became. I smiled and shook my head, wishing Lana didn't have to go anywhere as I walked into the bedroom.

Even though the bottom half of her was anchored, she was swinging her body, arms up in the air to the music.

I grinned. "I'm surprised you didn't belt this out at karaoke night."

"I thought about it." She fell back against the pillows when the song ended. Her fingers stopped the music from her phone, and she sighed.

"I found a half-eaten croissant on the comforter."

I smiled and sat down at the end of the bed. "Yeah. We were having a pretty deep conversation, and then the next thing I knew, you were out."

She giggled. "I don't remember any of that."

"You had a rough night and morning. I'm sure

you're exhausted."

Lana nodded and looked at the cast. "I can't believe I went hiking, horseback riding, canoeing, and even flew in a helicopter, all without a scratch. I try to walk down a set of stairs, and all bets are off."

"Yeah. You played it off well, though."

She focused her gaze on me. "How'd you know it was bad?"

I watched you talk to Grey and hobble out of the bar. I went over and asked him what you requested, and I wanted to find out about the best place to take you in the middle of the night."

Lana groaned. "What a way to end the best vacation in the world."

"And just think how it started," I teased, and she chuckled.

"Your manager really did look like Lars. What did you say his name was?"

"Ted, and I could definitely see the resemblance."

The doorbell rang, and my heart seized like an old truck rusted out in the middle of the field. I didn't want to move. I almost couldn't move.

"Remember, the doctor said that you guys should stop every couple of hours so you can get out and kind of move on your crutches."

She nodded.

I sucked in a deep breath. "This is rougher than I thought."

"Ditto." She hissed as she tried to move.

"Are you sure you should really be cooped up in your car for the next ten hours?" I stood to go to the door.

"No, but it's for the best. I need to get home somehow, and my car is here."

I nodded. "Don't move. Let me help you get up and ready."

She frowned and waved her hand in the air. "I've got it. I'm fine."

I shrugged and made my way to the door.

When I opened it, there wasn't one woman, but two. They looked nothing alike, one with brown eyes and the other with bright blue eyes, and their body shapes couldn't be more different.

"Are you Samantha and Vera?" I asked,

remembering her sisters' names.

The curvy one stepped forward. "Close. I'm Samantha, and this is Lana's half-sister, Charlotte."

"Oh, wow. Nice to meet you both."

Not sure Lana was expecting this surprise.

"Come on in. Lana's on the bed with her leg in the air. She's due for more pain meds soon," I explained. "The doctor wanted her to get out of the car every couple of hours."

Charlotte nodded. "Makes sense for blood clots."

"If there's anything I can do, let me know. I offered to charter a plane, but Lana wouldn't hear of it."

Samantha scowled and laughed. "Are you serious? I would have taken you up on that."

"She wouldn't even let me help get her out of bed and changed," I continued.

Charlotte howled as we walked into the bedroom. My eyes darted to see Lana completely naked on top, curled over her crutches, and shaking her booty to more eighties music.

For the life of me, I couldn't understand how this

happened. When I left the room, she was fully clothed in pajamas, which were now hanging off the bed.

"Hey." Lana smiled and then noticed Charlotte. "Wow. You didn't have to come too. That's so nice of you."

Charlotte grinned, composing herself. "It was my day off, and when Sam said she was going to try to make the drive nonstop, I had to help."

It was like none of us wanted to mention the elephant in the room, which were Lana's dangling breasts.

"Aww." Lana looked completely out of it. "That's so sweet of you guys. I'm all ready to go. I swapped my jammies for something cooler."

I glanced at Samantha, who was trying not to fall over in a fit of laughter, so I quickly grabbed one of my shirts and made my way over.

"I think what you have planned is a little too chilly for the ride home," I said, helping her to lean on me instead of the crutches as I pulled my shirt over her head. I anchored the crutches back under her arms, and she glanced down to see the shirt.

"Oops. I swore I'd put on a shirt. I would have bet my life on it."

"Good thing you didn't." I laughed as Lana's eyes stayed on mine for a few seconds too long. All it took was that extra moment to wish that there was something I could do to stop Lana from leaving.

But I understood. We'd barely met. Her recovery was going to be a long one. She needed her sisters and the comfort of the inn.

"Not to rush anything, but we should probably get on the road," Charlotte said as Samantha nodded.

"Grey packed everything and dropped it off this morning for Lana," I told them. "I loaded up the car already."

"You're a keeper," Samantha said, smiling as Lana looked over at me again. "You'll have to visit the inn while she's recovering."

I nodded, handing Samantha Lana's medications. "I'm planning on it."

Lana snapped her fingers as she managed to clutch the crutch. "I need some escargot."

Samantha rubbed Lana's back and grimaced.

"That might be hard to get at any I-90 rest stops."

I chuckled and nodded. "These pills do a number on her. She'll probably be out in ten minutes if you give her another one."

"I'm right here." Lana waved her arms as the crutches went flying, and her sisters quickly reached for them while I grabbed Lana.

"Yes, you are, and you're making it so we can't forget that."

Lana grinned and puckered her lips. "Kiss me, Cowboy. It might be your last shot at all of this."

I glanced at her sisters and shrugged. "It had better not be."

I slid a soft kiss against her lips.

"You know I haven't slept with many men, especially recently." Lana smiled, and Samantha snorted. "This was fun."

I eyed Samantha, and she couldn't keep in her laughter.

"A little TMI for the road never hurt anybody," I said, chuckling.

"Oh, I'll have way more for them."

"That's what I'm afraid of." I grinned as she started moving her crutches, swinging her leg, and making her move out of the house.

It was impossible to shake the dread that was slowly filling up every part of my body. This house had never been alive until Lana stepped inside. Kind of like how I felt as a person.

And now she was leaving.

I helped her to the car as her sisters opened the doors and adjusted the pillows I'd put in the back.

Lana stopped and looked into my eyes. "You've been really good for me, Jacob."

I kissed her without responding, hoping that would be enough to hold myself together.

CHAPTER NINETEEN

Lana

"And then this one time, we were on a hiking trail, and he pulled me into his arms, and the world started spinning," I explained. "Actually spinning. Another time, fireworks went off. I'm sure of it."

Samantha looked in the rearview mirror as Charlotte chuckled. "I thought Jacob said these things would knock her out."

I laughed and looked outside at the scenery speeding by, taking me away from the best time I'd ever had, and I knew I was making the wrong decision.

But it was the only decision I could make.

Jacob and I'd barely met. Sure, we'd slept together, but it wasn't like I could ask him to suddenly take care of me while I healed.

This was the right thing to do. I needed Cloudberry Inn.

"Thanks for coming, Charlotte," I said, feeling a little less loopy.

"Totally." Charlotte turned in the front seat and looked at me. "Anytime any of you need something, I'll always try to be there."

"It's really sweet of you."

She let out a deep breath. "It's the least I can do."

I chuckled. "You know we love you, right?"

Charlotte's smile deepened.

"Anyway, how's your dating life?" I continued. "We're the only two single sisters left."

Charlotte chuckled and turned back around to face forward. "My dating life is what you call nonexistent."

Samantha grinned. "Lana has never experienced that, have you?"

I'd always done an amazing job of implying things about my dating life over the years, probably since Lars, actually, in order for me to evade questions. My sisters probably thought I'd slept with a ton of men, but the truth was the exact opposite. The bonus of never correcting their imaginations was that I never endured endless questions. They always assumed that I was just a woman full of flings when the thought was actually terrifying.

"I'm sure we've all had our droughts." I kept my gaze out the window as the red rocks poked out of the jagged earth toward the brilliant blue sky.

"Yeah, right." Samantha smiled and glanced at Charlotte.

"Okay, total confession," I said suddenly. "You and Vera have always assumed that I'm experienced, but I'm the exact opposite. My dating life has been at a zero for most of my dating years. I just never corrected either of you when you assumed certain things."

Samantha gasped. "No way."

I nodded. "Yeah. For some reason, you always

thought I had a way with men, and since you were a bestselling author, I thought I had to have at least some sort of skill."

Charlotte snickered.

"You've made my day, Lana Roberts," Samantha said, grinning in the mirror.

"So, finding this musician is really quite a find," I added. "I mean, I've gone from zero to sixty pretty quickly."

Charlotte turned around again and nodded at me. "He is really nice. Granted, I've only met him for less than ten minutes, but he seems so charming."

"And charismatic," Sam added.

I nodded happily, thinking back to Jacob. He was both of those things and so much more.

"He has so much depth, and he can take a joke, which is good since I insulted his music before I knew it was his," I revealed.

"Ouch." Charlotte chuckled.

"Yeah. It should have been really bad, but it wasn't. Nothing has been with Jacob. We just kind of fit." I let out a sigh, feeling the throbbing rachet up in my leg. "Is it time for my medicine?"

"About ten minutes," Charlotte said, glancing at Sam. "But maybe it's okay to do it a few minutes early?"

"There's an exit up here. We can have you get out of the car and get your medicine."

I nodded. "I really wanted to finish out my vacation there."

"You can always go back," Samantha reminded me. "Amy's got a really great handle on things, and her sisters are really helpful too. You don't ever need to feel like you're stuck somewhere."

I smiled before another twinge of pain brought me back to reality.

"Hopefully," I said, grateful my sister had turned off the interstate. "But I don't know what to do other than be an innkeeper."

Samantha found a gas station that she quickly pulled into and parked. "Need anything?"

I grinned as Charlotte came around to help me out of the car. "I'd love some Ding-Dongs."

Samantha shook her head. "Seriously? I eat celery

sticks, and you can see where every one of them leaves a new roll or bulge, and you get to eat Ding-Dongs and look that stunning?"

Samantha always knew how to make me feel better.

I grunted and groaned my way out of the car with the help of Charlotte as Samantha wandered into the gas station. Charlotte handed me a soda and medicine, which I happily took.

"Even with a broken ankle, this trip home is a lot more fun than driving to Montana myself."

Charlotte secured the crutches under each arm. "I'm glad to hear it. It's nice to get to spend time with you. It's usually with Vera and the men and on and on."

I chuckled. "Yes, the men. They always bring the men."

She walked with me as I crutched my way to the front of the store and back.

"Do you believe in forever and after?" I asked Charlotte.

She looked startled at the question. "I don't

know."

I nodded. "Same. I used to."

Charlotte pressed her lips into a thin line. "Until my surprise?"

I laughed, feeling my leg throb as I made my way back to the car. "That might have warped my views a little."

She sighed and nodded, helping me slide back into the car with my legs across the entire backseat. "I'm sorry."

I straightened and grabbed her wrist. "Don't be. I'd much rather have a sister than a false sense of reality."

"Really?"

"One thousand percent." I thought back to my dad. "And something tells me my dad will feel the same way."

Her expression hardened. "I know. I need to tell him. I just—"

"You'll know when it's time," I said, letting go of her hand. "Just don't go too long. You never know how long any of us are gifted with the time here on Earth."

"For someone on a lot of medication, you're pretty perceptive."

I chuckled. "It's probably because of the medicine. The lips just keep smacking." I spotted my sister with a plastic bag with all sorts of goodies sticking out. "I'm in heaven. Looks like she got more than Ding-Dongs."

Charlotte closed the door and climbed back into the front seat as Sam piled into the car with our snacks.

"This should last us the next six hours." She glanced at the pumps. "I'll fill up too."

"Do whatever you want. Just hand over the Ding-Dong."

Samantha chuckled and gave me the entire bag of snacks, which was heaven in itself.

"I wonder what Jacob is doing?" I asked.

"Probably having flashbacks of your boobs hanging down while you were on crutches," Samantha teased.

"Please. My crutches covered me up."

Charlotte turned in her seat. "How do you

figure?"

"Well, I had them turned..." I frowned. "Oh, man. These pills are very bad."

"But at least they take the pain away," Samantha chimed in as she pulled up to the gas pump.

I shook my fist to the sky. "At what cost? At what cost? I have lost all dignity."

Samantha grinned as I took a bite of the delicious Ding-Dong. "You're a handful."

I shrugged and took another bite as I thought about Jacob. Was he poring over new lyrics? Did he remember me? It had been at least a few hours since I'd left him.

I let out a sigh as the gas pump clicked, and Samantha tapped it off before climbing back into the car.

"Washington, here we come," she said, turning the car on.

"Here we come," I said, dipping into the second Ding-Dong in the package.

I took a bite and let out a happy moan. "Do you know that Jacob Miller was in a boy band before he hit it even bigger as a country singer?"

"Why, yes, I did." Samantha grinned. "Vera had a poster of him when he was in that boy band."

"No. Way." My eyes widened.

Samantha laughed. "What if it's in storage?"

"I would die happily." I chuckled. "If, for some crazy reason, Jacob actually comes to visit me, I've got to find that poster."

"I'll help you look," Charlotte offered.

"Yeah?"

She nodded. "Or I can just try to hunt one down on eBay."

I chuckled, feeling a swarm of butterflies at the mere thought of Jacob's coming to the inn. I knew it was a long shot, but this entire encounter had been something of lottery odds.

I put the bag of snacks on the floor as my lids became heavy, and I propped my head against the seat and window. It wasn't exactly ideal, but the drowsiness didn't care.

"How, exactly, did you break your ankle?" Charlotte asked as I let out a big yawn.

"I had just finished singing a duet with Jacob, and when I was coming off the stage, I thought I saw Lars."

"The dead guy?" Charlotte asked.

I nodded. "I've got this thing for ghosts."

"We all do," Samantha explained. "Our mom was positive that Cloudberry Inn had ghosts."

"Mmm-hmm," I said softly, thinking back to the encounters I'd had over the years.

I couldn't say for certain that there weren't ghosts hanging out at the inn. There were plenty of odd things that happened, like pictures being hung on opposite walls by morning, creaks going up the stairs when there was no sign of anyone around, and lights flickering when I'd think back to my mom. Or we just had bored guests.

A lump suddenly formed in my throat, and I blinked my eyes closed. Being on narcotics for a broken ankle wasn't the time to start reminiscing.

"Anyway, it turned out to be Jacob's manager, but the damage had already been done. I'd lost my marbles in public and had to enjoy a trip to the emergency room."

Charlotte chuckled softly. "At least it was for a good cause."

"Yeah?" I said with my eyes still closed, tasting the bits of chocolate left behind from the Ding-Dong. "What's the cause?"

"Having a good time," Charlotte stated.

"Lana has always been one for having a good time. Even back in grade school," Samantha started. "I remember this one time, her friend got mumps, and Lana gathered all of her friends to serenade the mump girl in her front yard."

The memory made me smile. "I totally forgot about that."

"I didn't," Samantha said. "Any chance you had to sing when you were a kid, you did."

"Now it takes alcohol and a lot of coercion." I snuggled into the pillow, hoping it would take some of the uncomfortable pains away from being stuffed in the back of my car at such an odd angle. But after a lot of squirming, I realized it had nothing to do with the car. It was an awful gnawing in the pit of my stomach.

"Only you would take the term *break a leg* to the next level," Samantha said, turning on the radio to hear Jacob's voice sing one of his heartbreakers.

"Is this a sign?" I asked, blinking my eyes open.

"Only if you want it to be." Charlotte smiled, singing along with Jacob's music.

"I think I do."

CHAPTER TWENTY

Jacob

It had been precisely four days since Lana left Montana, and I'd been going through withdrawals since she'd left.

I'd texted her plenty of times, but I wanted to give her enough time to have made it to a few orthopedic appointments or whatever she needed to do to get situated.

But I couldn't handle it any longer.

My plane touched down at SeaTac two hours ago, and I was only ten minutes from the inn. I'd arranged to stay there with Samantha, and my visit was meant to be a surprise.

I just hoped the surprise was a good surprise. After all, I was on her turf, and last I'd heard, she'd had a few trysts with a gardener and a bellboy at the inn.

In Montana, she was on vacation without the everyday worries that she had back home. I could show up at the inn, and she has vacation remorse and chases me away.

But I doubted it or I wouldn't have boarded the plane.

I squeezed the steering wheel a little tighter as I turned down the road leading to the inn. I shouldn't be nervous, but I was.

I'd stood on stage in front of tens of thousands of people without a twinge of worry or anxiousness. But there I was, headed to a room of one, and beads of sweat were threatening to form under my hat.

I smiled to myself as the inn came into view.

It was absolutely perfect. I could see why it was hard for her to want to leave. I noticed several gardens leading up to the parking lot and scowled as

I thought about the lucky gardener. Hopefully, he wasn't up there taking care of Lana and having the time of his life.

"Get a grip, buddy," I whispered to myself as I turned off the truck and noticed a couple hand in hand wandering through some of the flowers.

Cloudberry was truly an idyllic place. I glanced at my bag in the backseat. I'd leave it in the car in case things went south and I had to hightail it out of there.

I drew a breath, climbed out of the car, and made my way to the front of the inn, where Samantha quickly threw open the door and motioned for me to hurry in. Her smile was warm and excited, which told me this could have been a great idea.

Samantha gave me a quick hug. "She won't shut up about you, and she's not on any pain meds, so I know it's real."

I laughed, and Samantha's finger zipped to her lips. "She has your music on replay, so I'm sure she'd recognize your laugh."

I nodded and smiled, seeing how much Samantha cared for Lana. She really wanted to make her sister happy, and that made me like Samantha even more.

"I told her that I'd bring up some tea. I thought that maybe you might deliver it?"

"Absolutely." I grinned, taking in the foyer that they'd turned into the lobby.

The old mansion had been beautifully restored over the years. It was obvious the place was loved. A huge floral arrangement had been set on a large circular table near a grand staircase.

"Okay, perfect." She motioned for me to follow her. "Right this way is the kitchen."

"Great."

We walked past what appeared to be an elevator. "I bet that's come in handy."

Samantha laughed. "Who knew we'd need it for our own sister?"

I chuckled. "How's she doing?"

"She's doing absolutely... awful." Samantha poured hot water over a teabag. "She's trying to act happy, but it's an act. She has this weird habit of plastering a phony smile on her face rather than just look how she feels."

I laughed softly and nodded. "I could see that happening. Is it her ankle that's got her bummed?"

My chest tightened, hoping I'd hear something to boost my ego.

"I don't think she even remembers she broke it. She's so focused on..." Samantha stopped herself. "I've probably said too much."

She handed me a tray with two cups of tea. "Just promise you won't break my sister's heart."

I looked into Samantha's eyes and nodded slowly. "I'll do everything in my power to make her happy."

"That's all I needed to hear." Samantha gave me directions to Lana's room and started toward the lobby but stopped. "I'd give you a room key, but I feel like you might not need your own."

I grinned and shook my head, realizing if this thing with Lana went anywhere, I'd have my hands full with all the sisters. I liked the thought as I carefully made my way up the stairs, but it made me think back to my parents. The family I already had.

When I found what I hoped was Lana's room, I slowly pushed the door open and nearly dropped the tea to the floor.

She was even more gorgeous than I remembered. The moment her gaze connected with mine, her happy spirit filled the room, and I knew I'd made the right decision.

A squeal rang through the air as she attempted to wiggle on the bed with her arms outstretched.

"Surprise!" I grinned, putting the tray down so we didn't add scalding burns to her list of injuries.

Before I had a chance to hug her, she was sniffling and snorting and crying.

"Is this a good cry?" I asked, kneeling next to the bed.

"Oh, yes." Tears fell down her cheeks as I carefully wrapped my arms around her.

"I've missed you so much," I said in between her sniffles.

"I'm probably stinky," she said, sniffling. "I've been using dry shampoo and sponge baths."

I laughed and hugged her harder.

"And if that doesn't scare you away, maybe we have a shot." She buried her runny nose into my neck, and I'd never felt something so good.

I breathed in everything about Lana and this moment.

"You smell powdery fresh," I teased.

"Good. That was the scent I was going for." She lessened her hug, and I backed up to take Lana in again.

"You're even more beautiful than I remember."

She giggled and tugged the blankets up a little. "But I remember your advice about setting the bar low, and then everything seems like an improvement or something like that."

I smiled, keeping her hands in mine. "I don't quite remember the conversation going like that, but I'm not one to argue with a patient."

"I can't believe you're here," she said softly, dabbing the tears away.

"I would have flown out the same day you left, but I thought that might be a little desperate looking."

Lana's smile only widened, and she let out a happy moan. "Let's not forget how we met."

"A funeral."

She nodded. "So, from this moment on, let's stop caring if we look desperate. If we're having the time of our lives, let's say it. Let's celebrate it."

"Lana, I'm having the time of my life."

She brought her hands up to my face and slowly traced her fingers along my cheek when I noticed something hanging on her wall.

Me.

At nineteen.

"You've got to be kidding me."

She chuckled and nodded. "My sister, who you haven't met yet, apparently loved every single thing about you. Charlotte found this old poster in our storage." I grinned. "And now I know why she was in such a hurry to put it up today."

I laughed and shook my head. "Genetics runs strong with your family. You all have a wicked sense of humor."

"Well, do you mind doing me a favor?" she asked.

"Sure."

"Can you peek out my window at the pool and make sure the pool boy isn't here?"

I cocked my head, completely surprised at the request, but I complied more out of shock than anything.

I pulled back the curtains and saw nothing but gardens.

"Wait a second. Cloudberry Inn has no pool?" I laughed and thought back to the front desk. "Or a bellboy?"

She winked. "But we do have a gardener."

"Should I be worried?" I teased, realizing Lana could weave stories with the best of them.

"Life will never be dull with you, will it?"

Lana scooted forward and turned around to get a good look at my teenage self. "What's that supposed to mean?"

"I've never smiled so much since meeting you and your sisters."

Lana pretended to flinch. "Well, you haven't met Vera yet. She's the real peach."

I smiled. "Yeah?"

"Oh, yeah. She'll kick ya in your teeth and watch you pick them up off the ground."

My eyes widened. "Seriously?"

Lana laughed. "No. She's gotten a lot nicer since she reunited with her long, lost love of a million years. Well, that and moving away from Cloudberry. I like her better in Silver Ridge."

A wicked laugh escaped my lips at her honesty. "She's the one who opened the bookstore?"

"Yup. Charlotte also has one, but hers is here in town." Lana drew a breath and glanced around the room as if someone could hear her. "I've never said this aloud, but it's been a real treat having Vera so far away." She flicked her wrists toward the ceiling. "Don't get me wrong. I love her to pieces, but it was just her and me for so long at the inn, and she hated every single second."

"And you?" I asked.

"I never stopped long enough to give it much thought."

I cupped her hands in mine. "Here's a theoretical question for you."

"I haven't taken the pain pills for quite a few days, but I don't know if I'm ready for anything too philosophical."

"If you had a million dollars in the bank, what would you do with your life? Would you stay at Cloudberry, or would you try something else?"

Lana blew air out of her pursed lips. It was hard not to bend over and kiss her mouth, but this was a serious question.

"I don't know." She looked around her room.

But that was it. This was Lana's room in an inn she took care of, day in and day out.

"Honestly, I stink at the business side of Cloudberry. If it hadn't been for Samantha, the inn could have faced some real problems." She sucked in a breath and let it out slowly. "My baking has gotten a lot better, but I'm not spectacular at it. I keep attempting to grow a green thumb, but that's not looking great, either." She wiggled her thumbs. "But Cloudberry is all I've ever known."

"Do you want to know something else?"

She nodded. "I would, but it would have to be handed to me at this point. I'm all out of ideas and surrounded by people who know exactly what they want."

"There's nothing wrong with just being happy." I scooped her hands back in mine. "Are you happy?"

Lana nodded. "I am. I truly am, but I'm even happier now that you're here."

"That's all that matters."

"I suppose." She looked conflicted. "I just feel like if I leave Cloudberry, will I have it to come back to, or will my sisters continue on with their own lives? The inn is the only thing that centers us. Even cranky Vera comes back now and again just to visit. If I weren't here, I'm not sure they'd take the time to visit me where I was."

Her words haunted me. Was that how my parents felt?

I nodded. "But that would be their loss, right?"

"I'd miss them. After my mom's death, when everything turned upside down and Samantha and Vera grew apart, it was torture for me. I'd always wondered if I were just too sensitive for my sisters. They could go weeks and months without talking, which could then turn into years." I shrugged. "And I

was always caught in the middle, so I just shut down."
I laughed. "Fun stuff, huh?"

"Families are complicated."

Now wasn't the time to elaborate on the fact that I hadn't been home to see my parents for a couple of years for the mere fact that I couldn't bear to go inside the house.

"What about you?" Lana asked. "You've heard me go on and on about my sisters. Do you have any siblings?"

My gaze fell to our hands laced together. "I do."

"Yeah?"

"Or I did. I had a sister, but she passed away."

Lana's hands flew to her mouth. "I'm so sorry."

I shook my head. "I still haven't figured out what to say after."

"After?" Lana asked.

I glanced around Lana's room, realizing how pure and happy everything in it was. I brought my gaze back to Lana's and nodded.

"Yeah, after someone tells me they're sorry for my loss. I just never know what to say. Like it's okay because it's not. I'm not okay. My family's not okay. Or do I just say thank you and move on? It's why I just don't tell anyone."

Lana scooted closer while balancing her cast on the mountain of pillows.

I started again. "Sorry. That was kind of a—"

"Shh." Lana draped her arms around my shoulders and rested her head there. "You have nothing to apologize for, and I certainly don't know what to say. Sometimes, silence is best."

As Lana hugged me, it felt like the weight of the world was slowly rolling off my shoulders.

After several minutes, she let her arms fall away and looked into my eyes.

"How did it happen?" Lana asked.

Rather than wanting to run away from the question, for the first time ever, I wanted to tell her everything.

The guilt I carried.

The sisterly love I never got to share.

The dreams we never got to experience together.

The family I turned away from.

And how it was all my fault.

CHAPTER TWENTY-ONE

Lana

"Everything was my fault," he said softly, dropping his gaze away from mine.

He set his cowboy hat next to us on the bed.

His statement wielded a power I didn't know could exist from mere words.

The pain etched in his gaze tore my heart wide open as I reached for his hand.

"I'm sure it wasn't."

He nodded and turned his gaze toward the window. "No, it was. If I hadn't started singing, she'd still be here."

Jacob's words were weighted with sorrow, and I

didn't know what to say.

"It had haunted me every single day." He took a deep breath. "Until I met you."

"I—thank you." I pressed my lips together. "But you didn't cause her to pass away. Why do you think that?"

Jacob brought his gaze to mine. "She got caught up in the darker side of the industry. It happened so fast, and none of us recognized the signs."

Horror outlined his features as if it had happened yesterday.

I squeezed his hand.

"That's not your fault."

He shrugged. "If I'd become a banker, she'd still be here."

"You don't know that."

He touched his chest and smirked, and I saw a more distant Jacob than I had before. "I do know it."

"Was it drugs?" I asked.

His gaze connected with mine. "Yeah. She went on tour with me. We'd begged my parents. I vowed to protect her."

"Oh, my God," I said softly, shaking my head.

"It was before I went solo. One of the guys in the band gave her something, and she liked it."

"I'm so sorry." My throat clenched with sadness as I watched Jacob relive the entire ordeal.

Jacob shook his head. "We were on tour the summer in between school years. She went off to college, and I went on tour. It was the summer after her freshman year."

"Did it take just that one time?"

He shook his head. "No. She got hooked. I didn't know it, but Neil kept her supplied. I thought the biggest thing I needed to worry about between those two would be her coming home pregnant."

"It's not your fault. You can't blame yourself," I said softly as my mind swirled in this revelation.

"But I can, and I do. If she'd just stayed home and partied like a normal college kid—"

"Someone else could have handed it to her, and the same outcome could have happened."

I leaned over and hugged him. "You can't spend the rest of your days blaming yourself for a choice she made."

He stiffened in my embrace.

"She was my little sister." His voice lowered, and he cleared his throat as he backed out of my arms. "I should have figured it out. I didn't notice the signs. I was too into being famous."

The pieces of the puzzle slowly started to click.

"Did it happen on the tour bus?" I asked.

"No. I almost wish it had. I could have been there for her. Evie died at my parents' house. She went back home to prepare for her sophomore year. She wanted to be a doctor." He squeezed his eyes shut, and he shook his head. "My parents found her in her bedroom, but it was too late. Neil must have given her some for the trip home."

Everything about Jacob's songs suddenly made sense. All the loss woven through his lyrics, all the heartache thrown into each verse, and the constant blame and self-condemnation finally all made sense.

His songs were his true story layered in musical riddles.

Jacob slid his wallet out and showed me a picture

of him hugging a girl not much younger than him. Her blonde hair was braided, her eyes bright with happiness. They looked so similar.

"She's beautiful," I whispered.

Jacob nodded and pulled out another picture. She was hanging on some guy. She looked vague and distant.

"And this was her at the end of that summer. How did I not see it? I could have sent her to rehab or had Neil arrested." He shook his head. "How did I not recognize it?"

"You can't shoulder this, Jacob. It's easy to look back and see a decline, but those summers are built on people changing and finding themselves."

"Or losing themselves." His eyes met mine, and I nodded.

"She made a choice, though."

"But she was so young and impressionable." His frown deepened. "I didn't protect her."

"We all are. We all were. It doesn't mean we all try a drug we're handed." I drew a breath and waited a couple of seconds. "Did you do drugs?"

Jacob's eyes darkened. "No. I haven't even smoked weed."

"There you go."

Jacob kept looking at me, and I suddenly felt like I'd overstepped my bounds.

"I'm not trying to sound like a coldhearted b—"

He reached his hand to my cheek, stopping me from continuing. "You're not."

I cupped his hand as it slid off my face. "Thank you."

"It's been a long, hellish journey. I didn't just lose my sister. I lost my parents. The thought of going back to the same house where she overdosed..." He shook his head. "I've begged my parents to let me buy a new home for them, but over fifteen years later, they still won't budge."

"They probably feel like that house still holds her spirit. The last place they can be close to her."

I knew I felt that way with Cloudberry Inn. Some days, that was good, and other days, not so much.

"I'm sure that's it," he said quietly. "But I can't face going there. I just can't. When it first happened, I came home the moment I'd heard. My father lunged at me. It took my uncle to hold him back. I remember his finger in my face, his telling me I'd killed her."

I gasped at the words, and my heart pulled in so many directions.

"Jacob, you didn't deserve that."

"My dad told me not to come to the funeral. Told me he had people to make sure I didn't get in."

I breathed a slow breath.

"I still went."

"You have been to hell and back."

"My parents look at the money I've made like it's dirty. Like it took their daughter from them."

"I feel like you look at it like that too."

He shrugged. "Maybe."

"I had no idea." I shook my head. "You've never mentioned much about your family."

"I love my parents, and I wish we were closer, but that's not how things worked out."

I nodded, thinking back to my dad. Once he left for Arizona, we'd all grown a little distant, but hearing about Charlotte, her mom, and the affair put a pretty thick wall up around me. It all felt like such a betrayal, and I didn't know how to act as if I didn't know any of the dirty details of my dad's other life. I couldn't unhear the details. I couldn't unlearn what he'd done to my mom.

Jacob's gaze stayed on mine. "Thanks for listening."

"I just wish I could take the pain away, Jacob."

"I've been searching for that too." He slid closer to me. "I'd given up hope. Kind of thought my life would always be miserable and lonely. Then I met you."

"Jacob—"

He ran his hand along my head, pulling me into him. Our foreheads touched, and I felt closer to him than I had to anyone.

"I missed you from the moment you left Montana." He sat back and smiled at me. "It hasn't even been a week, and I miss you like I've been on the road for six months, yet it's only been days."

I smiled. "I tend to do that to people. They just can't get enough of me."

Jacob laughed, the sadness in his gaze drifting

away. "See? That's what I love. You ground me in the reality of now, not what's going on up here." He pointed at his head.

"I've felt something special with you too. For the first time, I feel like I could be myself. I don't think twice about what comes out of my mouth." I smiled. "Maybe I should, but I don't."

A twinge of pain darted through my ankle, and I readjusted. "But I can't lie and say I'm not worried about this leading to a dead end."

Jacob nodded slowly.

"I'm so scared to give it my all and then find out we can't make it work." I shifted my weight to get a better look at Jacob. "The truth of the matter is that you're a musician. You're on the road or in the studio. You live in Montana. I help run an inn, not in Montana. I don't see how this could work."

Jacob nodded. "And I don't see how it could not work. I can live wherever I want. Before I met you, I'd decided to hang up my hat."

"No pun intended," I teased about his cowboy hat.

"Right. See? I need this, Lana. I need to see if we

can make this work." He glanced at my cast. "How it's feeling?"

"Much better except if it twists in my cast or something." I looked out the window for a few seconds and wondered if there was a way to make it work.

"What are you thinking?" Jacob asked.

"I'm wondering if I could ever leave Cloudberry Inn." I sat back on the pillows. "It's not like I know how to do anything else. I'm comfortable here. I don't mind working here, especially now that someone has taken over the business side of things."

Jacob nodded.

"I've just never allowed myself to think of something else." I let out a heavy sigh. "I've always fit neatly packaged in this box. I've even got the customer-service grin down to a science."

"But are you happy?" Jacob asked. "When you see yourself at eighty at Cloudberry Inn, are you happy?"

"I'm not unhappy," I said softly, knowing I'd given this so much thought over the years and never came up with something else.

"Well, I don't want to be the one to pull you away from a place you love."

I nodded, feeling a gnawing in my stomach. It was the same feeling as when I'd found out about Lars.

"I know, but it's a place. You're a person. You make me extremely happy. I just don't know if it's because I was on vacation or if it's real."

Jacob smirked. "I think you know."

I couldn't help but smile. "Yeah, I know. I just didn't want to sound like the crazy one."

"I think we might have a shot," he said, his eyes anchoring me in place. "We don't have to rush it. You don't have to have all the answers."

"That's good because I can guarantee that's not happening." I smiled, twisting my fingers with his as I pulled him closer. "How long are you planning on staying?"

"I didn't set a time limit."

"Music to my ears."

"As long as I'm not the one singing it, huh?"

I giggled and pulled him closer. "I love your music, and now I understand it."

Jacob smiled and placed a kiss against my lips, sending a wave of desire through me. I knew I'd do whatever it took to see if this thing could work between an innkeeper and a country music star.

Jacob's phone rang, and he quickly pulled it out of his pocket.

His face fell the moment he saw the number.

"It's my parents," he whispered before answering the call.

Within seconds, I knew something had happened, and there wasn't a thing I could do about it.

CHAPTER TWENTY-TWO

Jacob

"You've always risen to the occasion, Jacob. It's us who've failed you." My mom nodded slowly and looked over at my father.

Tubes and oxygen led away from his body with nothing but a hospital gown covering him.

"If I could have traded places with Evie, I would have in an instant," I revealed.

My mom gasped, and tears filled her gaze as she quickly shook her head and stood from her chair to reach me.

"You are no less valuable, no less important to us or this world than your sister, and shame on us for ever giving you that idea." My mom's expression turned stern. "I've always been angry at your father for the way he handled things with you. Her death wasn't something any of us could have predicted, but it certainly wasn't anyone's fault. Actually, no, that's not true. Her death was her fault."

My mouth parted, but I didn't know what to say.

Evie didn't mean to die.

"I know that sounds awful, but she made the choice to do something that altered all of our lives, and she didn't make it to see how much it screwed us all up." My mom nodded. "They say there are all those stages of grief, but I'm pretty sure I never left the stage of anger."

"I miss her so much, Mom. I try not to let myself wonder what she'd be doing today, or I go down a rabbit hole I can't jump out of."

"I know, babe." My mom cupped my face like when I was a little boy. "I do that too."

"Remember she wanted to be a doctor?" My breath caught.

"I do remember that." My mom let out a deep

breath.

"If I hadn't let her come on that tour, she might be here treating Dad." I looked over at my dad and felt a heaviness deep in my chest.

My mom's expression fell, and she shook her head. "I don't believe that to be the case."

Her words shocked silence right into me.

My mom glanced at my dad. "They promise me that he's in an induced coma and can't hear." She let out another deep breath. "Evie struggled with substances since she was fourteen. I caught her sneaking those little airplane bottles of booze in ninth grade. I promised not to tell your dad. Unfortunately, it didn't stop there." My mom folded her arms over her chest. "Do you remember that summer she went away to camp for about thirty days?"

The world around me froze.

"She wasn't at camp. She was in rehab at the age of sixteen."

"For what?" My pulse raced with this information.

"Drugs and alcohol. The details don't matter

now."

My heart stammered. "Why didn't you tell me? I never would have had her come on tour with me."

"Your father didn't know, either." She chewed on her bottom lip for a split second. "I thought she'd gotten over it. I thought it was fine."

"What?" A jolt of anger darted through me. "Dad didn't know his own daughter had a problem?"

"Evie begged me not to tell him. She was always Daddy's little girl. She promised me she would never touch anything again if I just kept it to myself. I believed her."

"Why wouldn't she have told me?" I asked, my voice hoarse.

"She never wanted to disappoint you. She adored you, and I truly believed in my heart that she'd had nothing more than a blip in her short life. We all make mistakes. If your father had found out, I don't know what he would have done. I don't know that she would have gotten a second chance."

But she might still be alive.

I rubbed my forehead and tried to make the

sudden headache go away. "I'm speechless."

My mom nodded. "I'm sorry I didn't tell you sooner."

Darkness had been right in front of me for years. It surrounded my every thought. I'd been close to touching it, embracing it, but I resisted. I refused to let myself fade away and let the darkness consume me.

I looked at my mom. Her eyes were filled with a recognizable pain, and I already knew what it felt like to live with this type of guilt.

I held out my arms, and she moved into my embrace as we rocked back and forth.

"Evie was a bright spirit." I hugged my mom. "She made every day a better one, and it's probably better that Dad never knew."

My mom nodded in my arms as dampness soaked my shirt.

"She loved so hard," my mom whispered. "She lived so hard in her short little life. I think that's why I kept this from you. I didn't want anything to tarnish your image of her."

I squeezed my mom tighter and shook my head. "Nothing could change how I feel about my little sister. She left the earth too soon, but I think she's been orchestrating things from above for years."

My mom sniffled. "You do?"

"Yeah. I do." I let go of my mom and debated what to say about Lana, if anything.

A doctor walked in, his eyes falling to my mom, who'd obviously been crying.

"I have some good news," the physician announced. "The fall doesn't appear to have done any serious damage. His MRI has come back clear. No sign of swelling. He has a slight concussion, and of course, the broken ankle from the tumble."

I nodded, feeling relief spread through me. "So, the sedation?"

"We sedated him because he was extremely agitated and refused treatment." The physician looked surprised that I didn't know all the details, but he obviously wasn't familiar with our family dynamic.

I turned to my mom and raised my brows. "You failed to mention that part."

"There's a lot of wheels turning."

"How long will he need to stay in the hospital?" I asked.

"I suggest that he goes to a rehab facility with his ankle unless you have the ability to take care of him."

I looked at my mom and sighed.

"I don't think my dad would be thrilled to go to a nursing home, no matter how short the stay. I'll be at the house."

My mom clapped her hands together, and I gritted my teeth while nodding.

"Okay, then I think we can get him released by tonight if all goes well today."

"Great." My mom beamed. "Such great news. Thank you, Doctor."

He nodded. "The nurse will come in with discharge information and the name of at-home therapy services. Any questions?"

My mom shook her head. "No, I think we'll be okay. We can always Google things."

The doctor flinched, and I reminded myself not to have my mom at any of my bedside care. I watched him leave and turned back to my dad. He had several lacerations along his cheekbone and eyes. I can see why they checked him out so thoroughly

"It's such a relief," my mom said, taking a seat next to my dad as the nurse came in.

She started disconnecting his IV and removing tubes. "He should start to awaken in the next hour or so."

My mom nodded as the nurse checked his blood pressure and rolled the IV station out of the room.

"So, Dad was a pain when he got here?"

My mom nodded. "It wasn't good. He was very unhappy. I can't even imagine what would happen if he thought he might have to go to a nursing home."

"Dad didn't use to be crabby." I studied my dad.

He looked so much older and quite frail. Granted, no one looked their best lying in a hospital bed, but I really saw a difference since the last time I saw him. My chest tightened at the thought.

My mom nodded.

"I remember as a kid thinking how lucky I was to have the dad I had. So many fathers were grouchy and snippy, and I always had the dad with the smile, throwing the baseball, and interested in hearing about our days." I cleared my throat. "He'd been so proud of me when I first hit it big."

"He's still proud of you," my mom said softly.

"I don't know about that," I stated flatly.

"Your dad changed after Evie."

"Haven't we all?" I let out a deep sigh. "I'm not here to argue or point fingers. I'm happy to be here however I can help."

"I'm sure after a couple of days, your dad and I will get into a routine, and you can go back to California."

I shook my head. "My house in San Francisco is under contract. I put it up for sale."

Surprise washed over my mom's face. "You did?"

I nodded. "Yeah. I've been giving a lot of thought to what I want to do with the rest of my life. I'm tired of being on the road by myself."

"I'm sure it's a lonely life. Well, maybe not for a lot of musicians, but if you're a loner to begin with, it can't be good."

I laughed. "A loner?"

"Don't act surprised. You were always the boy with a guitar sitting in the yard by yourself or staying in on the weekends to practice."

I snorted. "Geez. Way to make me sound like a loser."

My mom chuckled. "I wouldn't call anyone with the number of hits you've had a loser."

"Just a loner." I smiled. "Could be worse."

"I've often wondered if you would have been more receptive to opening your heart up if Evie had still been here."

I nodded. "Without a doubt, but I'm not sure I would have met the right person."

My mom's brows shot up. "Yeah? You think you have now?"

"I think I might have met my match."

"Why's the doctor talking about his love life?" my dad barked from the bed.

I walked closer, hoping to come into my dad's view.

"That's Jacob, dear. Not the doctor."

I was half expecting alarms to go off or something, but he just grunted and fell back asleep.

I looked over at my mom and took a deep breath. "Maybe the nursing home still has openings."

My mom chuckled, and I wondered if we might be on the path to a little bit of healing.

CHAPTER TWENTY-THREE

Lana

"I feel like my chains are starting to break free one at a time," I confessed to Samantha.

She looked surprised. "I didn't know you felt chained up."

We were sitting in the kitchen of the inn. I'd only heard from Jacob once since he'd left, but it sounded like his dad was going to get to go home.

"I didn't know I did, either." I smiled, looking down at my cast. "But something about Jacob makes me view life differently."

"Pretty special, isn't it?"

I nodded, realizing how close I'd become to Samantha since she'd come back to the inn. "It's amazing, actually."

"I thought I was completely content writing about the perfect love in my books. In fact, I was so certain of it that I shut down any attempt at it for years."

"Same. I've been so busy telling myself how content I am here at Cloudberry, I've let an entire decade slip by." I thought back to Jacob. "But I don't think any other man would have done it for me. It took this moment in time. It took Jacob."

"Exactly. We can try to question why we did things a certain way, but the truth is that we're here where we are now because of where we've been. Had you paid your bill on time to Garrett, I never would have met him."

I chuckled. "Well, I'm glad my less-than-expert bookkeeping skills changed your life."

She grinned. "In more ways than one."

"Hey, now." I playfully swatted at her as she backed away.

"Want some more tea?"

"That would be great."

"Well, too bad," she joked.

I rolled my eyes. "Remember how we did that to Vera when she sprained her ankle?"

Samantha snorted. "Oh, my gosh. And we wonder why she's the grumpy one?"

I grinned. "We hid them on her every time she turned around, and she had to hop everywhere."

"Poor Vera."

"Or we did it to her because she was always grumpy, and it was fun to poke the bear."

Samantha smiled wider. "Yeah, we just turned her into a grizzly."

"She has gotten better, though, don't you think?"

"Oh, yeah. Aside from the fact that Drew North is an actual saint of epic proportions, she's mellowed out a lot."

"I think it's safe to say she was truly miserable here," I said, shaking my head. "See, that's the thing. I've never felt miserable here or like I need to escape. Quite the contrary. At times, the thought of leaving

Cloudberry scares me to death."

My sister set the cup of tea in front of me. "But is it really the thought of leaving Cloudberry that scares you, or is it more about what's out there that scares you?"

I scowled. "I don't know what's out there."

"Exactly my point. I think it's the unknown that scares you more than the idea of leaving Cloudberry."

I nodded. "Could be. I've never been one who loved change." A grin spread across my face. "Except the idea of leaving Cloudberry hasn't been quite as scary."

Samantha took a sip of tea and nodded. "A little hunch tells me that has something to do with a certain someone named Jacob Miller.

I blushed. "Probably. Maybe. Could be. I plead the fifth."

"It was pretty incredible that he came out here to see you so soon after you left Montana."

I nodded, feeling warm all over.

My sister eyed me. "You do believe what he told you about his dad, though."

"Is that a question?"

"I guess."

My eyes widened. "Yeah. Totally. Why wouldn't I believe it?"

"Okay. Just checking. Must be the older sister vibe."

"But you're my younger sister."

She laughed. "True."

"I know in terms of length of time, we haven't spent that much time together, but—"

Samantha shook her head. "Not true. How many hours a day do you think you hung out?"

I smiled, thinking back to the amazing days and nights. "Probably eight or twelve or more."

"Or more." Samantha laughed. "Think about it. Most people only have snippets of time here and there when they start dating, and it's spread over weeks and weeks. I bet it's the equivalent of dating for like eight or ten weeks, at least."

I laughed. "You're such a writer."

"It's true," she assured me. "You guys know one another a lot better than most people who've been on a few dates."

I didn't know if it were true, but it felt like it. When I thought about Jacob, it was as if he were part of all my stories, like he'd somehow hovered in the background. It wasn't that we didn't share that newness and freshness of a blossoming relationship, but there was this comfort that I barely had with my family, let alone a man I'd only recently met.

"When Jacob was leaving, he mentioned something about hoping to sing a duet with you?"

I nodded. "Yeah. He wrote a beautiful song. It's the one I sang with him at karaoke right before I broke my ankle."

"I'd like to hear it."

I shook my head and took a sip of tea. "No way. It's a duet. It takes two of us."

"You have an amazing voice. I don't know why you get all shy."

"Because I'm a grown woman who might belt a tune out in the shower or car, but that doesn't mean I'm at Jacob's caliber."

Samantha shrugged. "Don't sell yourself short."

I laughed. "That's just it. I'm not selling myself at all."

Samantha smiled and shook her head. "You're impossible."

"You know, I've been thinking a lot about Dad lately."

Samantha's eyes settled on mine. "Yeah?"

I nodded. "And this Charlotte situation. I just... I just think she needs to tell him."

Samantha flinched.

"You don't think so?"

Samantha sighed and nodded. "No. I do, but it's not our place."

"I thought that several months ago, but how long is Charlotte going to let this go on? I thought she was going to tell him in the first month or two, maybe three, but it's been how long?"

Samantha nodded slowly. "I think she just wanted to make sure she had a solid foundation with us first. You know, we're her only family, in a sense."

"I get that. I just don't want something to happen to Dad, and he never knew." I attempted to adjust my bad foot and groaned in annoyance. "I'm so looking forward to showering with my foot in a garbage sack again. So much fun."

"Hey, you're the one who thought you saw a ghost."

I grinned. "Don't you ever wonder?"

Samantha leaned over the table slowly. "I do, but I'm not sure that's great for business."

I nodded in agreement as my cellphone rang.

Panic darted through me when I saw it was Jacob trying to FaceTime me.

"Oh, no."

"What?"

"It's Jacob on FaceTime." I ran my fingers through my tangles.

"Just go for it. If he can't handle the heat, he can get out of the kitchen."

"I'd like to wait until at least another month or so before I completely scare the man off," I teased.

"You look fantabulous. Now, just answer the phone and give me a holler when you want me to help get you in the shower."

I turned to my sister and smiled. "Thank you. I owe you one, yet again."

"I never keep score."

"Thank God for that," I mumbled as I answered his call.

"Hey, gorgeous," Jacob said.

His video popped onto my screen, and I immediately felt all gushy inside. How in the world had he cast his spell over me?

"Don't judge. I haven't showered yet. It's somewhat of an ordeal right now."

"You could be wearing a trash bag and look sexy."

"I'm glad you feel that way because in a few minutes, I'll be wearing one."

"Boy, you turn my days right around," he said, smiling.

"I was thinking the same thing. How's your dad?"

"He's doing really well." Jacob nodded slowly. "Surprisingly well. I guess when he first got to the hospital, he was so grumpy that they had to sedate him while they ran tests."

"Sounds like my sister Vera."

Jacob laughed and shook his head. "I can't wait to meet her."

Just hearing that he wanted to be more involved in all facets of my life did all kinds of crazy things inside me, like give me hope.

"I'll be here a few days or weeks. I don't know yet. Kind of depends on how much of a hard time he gives my mom. I'm not sure if he's going to be the best patient. He already refused his pain meds until he was in so much pain, he had to beg for them."

"Yikes."

"Fun times."

"How are you doing being back at the house?" I asked.

He let out a long sigh and nodded slowly as he looked into the phone. "Better than I thought. There's been a lot of healing, and not all from the places I expected."

"Really?"

He nodded. "I'll have to tell you when I see you again."

"That would be nice."

"I miss you," he said softly.

I groaned. "Me too. I've been trying to play it cool, but I got really attached to seeing your face every single day."

His grin only widened.

"I even miss your cowboy hat," I added.

"No kidding."

I nodded. "In fact, I thought you could send me a few special shots with your hat and nothing else."

A coy grin spread across his lips. "You do know that's how celebrities get in trouble, right?"

An evil laugh erupted from my lips, and I nodded. "Maybe it will keep you in check."

"Or skyrocket my career."

"I think your britches are big enough, Jacob Miller."

He smiled and was quiet for a few seconds as he contemplated something.

"Hey, do you want to meet my parents?"

My jaw dropped open. "Looking like this?"

"You're perfection, and my dad is heavily medicated. I doubt he'll remember."

I chuckled and nodded. "You know what? Sure."

"Great. I'll be right back."

I nodded, looking around the kitchen, when I realized that Samantha snuck off with my crutches. Even if I wanted to hobble my way to the bathroom to try to do something about the state I was in, I couldn't.

Jacob came back into view, and I saw a glimpse of who I thought was his mom behind him.

"Okay, I'm bringing the phone into the family room where my dad is on the couch. He's up but a little loopy."

Jacob seemed like a kid in the candy shop as he made his way to the family room.

"Okay, Mom and Dad. I know it's been a long time coming, but I have someone I'd like you to meet." Jacob's smile widened as his mom and dad came into view. "This is my girlfriend, Lana Roberts."

The word *girlfriend* rattled around my head like a tin can lid. Had I not been staring at his mom and dad, I probably would have had a wonderful out-of-body experience.

"Oh, honey. It is truly nice to meet you. Jacob told

me all about you. I'm so sorry about your ankle."

I glanced down at my cast and back at the screen, trying to smooth my hair down that was reflecting in the video. "Thank you. I'm not the most graceful of human beings."

His mom snickered. "Apparently, that runs in both families."

I saw his dad's wobbly head crane to the side as he tried to get a glimpse of me.

"You're just absolutely beautiful," his mom continued.

"I feel like a wreck. I'm back at my inn, but I can only shower with the help of my sister, and she's been busy hiding my crutches on me rather than helping me shower."

"Are you serious?" Jacob turned the camera to him.

"Yes. There are days I wonder if I live at a looney bin rather an old, distinguished inn."

Jacob laughed. "Let me have you say hi to my dad before he fades out."

I nodded. "Okay."

Jacob positioned the phone, and I saw his dad laid up on the couch with a pile of pillows that looked eerily similar to my own predicament.

"It's nice to meet you, Mr. Miller."

He squinted his eyes at me and moved his head in closer.

"Evie, is that you?" his father said, pointing at the screen.

I sat horrified when Jacob stepped in and his mom started shaking her head.

"No, Dad. That's my girlfriend, Lana."

"Not her. I know that's not my daughter, but Evie is standing behind her, smiling."

A chill ran across me as three pairs of eyes stared through me, searching for the impossible.

CHAPTER TWENTY-FOUR

Jacob

"You know, I say if you can't scare them off by being a musician on the road all the time, pull out the crazy card." I laughed, shaking my head at my mom.

"Oh, honey." My mom smiled. "She seemed very good-natured about the whole thing."

"Well, what else is she going to do?"

"I'm sure she understands that your dad is on a lot of medication."

"You want to know something even crazier?" I asked my mom.

"What?"

"I believed him."

My mom's expression softened as she reached for my hand. "I did too. I think we're all desperate to connect with the one thing that divided us all."

I let out a deep sigh, knowing that was the logical way of looking at it, but I wasn't so sure I was a very logical person.

I wanted to believe my dad saw Evie behind Lana, guiding our encounter, giving us the sign that it was okay, that Evie was okay.

My dad coughed in the other room, and my mom and I exchanged a glance.

"I'll go check on him," I told her.

"Sure. Dinner's almost ready."

I smiled at my mom and nodded. "Thanks."

"Well, we have to eat."

I laughed and walked into the family room where my dad was up and arguing with the news on the television.

"Feeling better?" I asked, sitting on the ottoman in front of him.

"I am." He glanced at me and pointed at the television. "Can you believe this?"

I scanned the screen and smiled.

My dad ripped his gaze from the news. "I know what I saw, Jacob."

I clasped my hands together and nodded. "I believe you."

His gaze narrowed on mine as if he were waiting for an argument. "You do?"

"I do. Mom came up with a logical explanation."

"And?" my dad prompted.

"I'm okay with not having all the answers."

My dad smiled, nodding. "It's nice to have you here."

"I wish it were under different circumstances."

My dad shrugged. "Could be worse."

I laughed. "Yeah. It can always be worse."

"You know, I might have been drugged up a storm in the hospital, but I feel like I heard you and your mom talking about everything that happened."

I froze, hoping he hadn't heard what my mom had revealed. I had been shocked my mom didn't tell him at the time everything went down with Evie, but I'd happily be the scapegoat now rather than have my mom decide to confess everything now and have my dad mad at her.

"You know, my biggest regret in life is how I handled things with you." My dad's gaze stayed on mine. "It was no more your fault than mine or your mom's. You didn't deserve any of what I said or did to you."

"I..."

No words would come.

"I'm beyond proud of you for what you've accomplished. It's astonishing the charts you've climbed and the level head you've kept on your shoulders."

"Thank you."

He grabbed my hand and tugged it toward him. "No, I mean it. Parents aren't always right. We're human, and we can make huge mistakes. Unfortunately, it can take some of us longer than others to realize when we've made a mistake."

I nodded, feeling a strange release roll through me.

"I would never trade one child for another, and

I'm truly grateful you're here." My dad shook his head and dabbed tears away. I'd only seen him cry one other time, and that was at Evie's funeral.

"I wish I had known."

My dad shook his head. "I think we've all learned how unhealthy secrets can be."

I realized then that my dad heard what my mom had revealed and had no intention of bringing it up.

"Let's work on the here and now." My dad winced as he tried to adjust on the couch.

"Do you need help?"

"Nah, I got it. Do you think I spooked your girlfriend?"

I laughed. "Something tells me it might take more than that to scare her off."

"She had quite the hair." My dad chuckled.

"Yeah. She's pretty beautiful. You know, she's in the same predicament as you. She broke her ankle getting off the stage with me."

"Oh? She's a performer?"

I laughed, thinking back to the situation. "No, she'll perform under extreme duress or alcohol."

My dad chuckled.

"But she has a beautiful voice. I could tell Ted wanted to sign her on the spot."

"Really."

I nodded.

"You know, I never liked that guy," my dad revealed.

"I know. It's why I told him I'd handle it."

"Do you think we'll get to meet Lana?"

"I sure hope so. I'm kind of hoping to convince her to record a duet with me."

"You should."

"It'll be up to her."

"Did you meet her on tour?"

"No, I've learned that lesson more than once."

My dad chuckled. "But wasn't it kind of a fun lesson to learn?"

I grinned and shook my head. "Not as fun as you'd think."

"Probably true."

"Mom said dinner will be ready soon, but I'm going to go call Lana."

"Please give her my apologies."

I nodded. "Mom said you were super loopy on your medication."

"She's right, but I stopped taking it."

"Again?"

My dad nodded, and I rolled my eyes on the way out of the family room.

He was as stubborn as they come.

I made my way upstairs and walked toward Evie's bedroom on the way to my old room, but instead of walking by, I stopped and opened the door.

I didn't know what to expect. Part me of thought my mom might have left it exactly as it had been. To me, it seemed like the entire house was a time capsule.

But when I opened the door, my sister's old bed had been traded out for a floral couch where several stacks of magazines had been scattered along with one of the cushions. The desk from my sister was still in the room, but all the stickers had been removed, and a magnifying lens sat squarely in the middle.

I stepped inside, expecting a crushing weight of

sorrow and regret to sweep over me, but it never came. My hand ran along the wall that had long since been painted, and I realized that maybe it was only me who'd been stuck in the past.

Sitting on the couch, I dialed Lana's phone and was surprised to see her answer from a steamy bathroom.

"Hello?" she said between huffs and puffs.

"Hey, I can call back," I suggested, wishing the camera lens would go just a little lower.

"Nah. That's okay. I lost all dignity about three hours ago after having to crawl to the bathroom when my sister forgot that she hid my crutches from me."

I couldn't stop laughing. "I'm so sorry."

Lana laughed. "It sounds like it."

"I'm not sure who needs me more. You or my dad."

"I'm just going to set the phone on the counter. We should be able to talk."

I watched her hop to the counter and then spin around with her tush to the camera as she hopped once toward the shower.

"Are you trying to torture me?" I asked, seeing her beautiful body maneuver into the shower.

"Cowboy, if you're getting turned on by a woman wearing a trash bag on her leg, you've got some serious problems," she said with her eyes shut as she scrubbed shampoo into her hair.

"Seriously? How can I not get turned on by a beautiful woman glistening with suds floating down her body?"

Lana chuckled, keeping her eyes shut. "Just think. It could be you helping me shower."

I grinned and shook my head. "Sign me up."

She reached for a washcloth and opened her eyes as she scrubbed her arms.

"Can you get any more beautiful?" I sighed into the phone.

"Well, give me a minute when I don't feel like a wet poodle, and we'll see."

"Since I have you on the line, I kind of want to bring something up."

"Uh-oh. Sounds serious."

"Not at all." I had to focus on the towel hanging

near the shower. "I know you've got a lot on your mind, but I'd like to add one more thing to the list."

"Sounds perfect."

"I know I brought this up right before you broke your ankle, but I was really serious."

"All I remember right before I broke my ankle was mistaking your manager for Lars."

I laughed. "Well, at least it's not just my family who sees ghosts."

She smiled as she scrubbed behind her ears. "Refresh my memory."

"We've kind of touched on it here and there, but..." I licked my lips. "I would love it if you would record the duet with me."

She stopped scrubbing. "I don't know the first thing about how to do that."

"You've proven you can sing. We can do the rest."

She turned to look into the phone and suddenly covered her breasts with the washcloth. "Who's we?"

"My manager and me. I'd say mostly me, but the truth is that Ted never wants to miss a payday."

"Wow. Boy, I don't know what to say." She shook

her head. "That's a lot."

"You don't have to give me an answer right away." I wished I hadn't said a word. "You'd be compensated."

Ooph. I wish I hadn't said that at this moment, either.

She turned off the shower and reached for a towel.

"Sorry. Now wasn't the time to bring it up."

Lana smiled and wrapped her towel around her as her sister came in.

"No, it's okay," Lana said.

"What's okay?" Samantha asked.

Lana pointed toward the counter. "Jacob is on the phone."

"Wait. Was I interrupting something? Oh my gosh. I'm so sorry. I—"

Lana started laughing. "No, it's nothing like that. We were talking business."

Samantha's brows rose. "Business?"

Why did I feel the need to bring up the duet while Lana was naked in the shower?

"Dinner," my mom hollered from downstairs.

As if things couldn't get worse.

"Oh, dinner?" Lana asked.

I nodded. "Yeah. I should probably head down."

Samantha could barely keep that smile off her face as she helped Lana out of the shower.

"No rush on an answer on that, Lana," I mumbled.

"Okay. I'll think about it." Lana waved at the phone.

"Think about what?" Samantha asked while I stood from the couch.

"Singing a song with Jacob."

"Okay, I'll call you tomorrow, Lana."

"Will you be sending me that photo with the cowboy hat we talked about?"

I hung up the phone and knew I was utterly doomed.

CHAPTER TWENTY-FIVE

Lana

Charlotte opened a box and squealed in delight. I hobbled over on my crutches and peered down into a fanciful box of colors.

"He's coming for a signing." Charlotte took out a book and waved it in front of me.

"Who is it? I can't see with as much as you're waving it around."

"My all-time favorite author," Charlotte gushed. "I'll be right back. "I'm just putting most of these in the back room for the event."

I nodded and found a loveseat near the window. Charlotte's bookstore really fit her. It was cozy and welcoming and crammed with books, magazines, and stationery.

It had been several days of roaming Cloudberry Inn on crutches and wondering when I'd be able to wander the grounds on two feet. Thankfully, Samantha had errands to run and dropped me off at Charlotte's bookstore.

"Okay, I'm back." Charlotte smiled, walking over to where I'd found a place to sit. "The events are so good for business, but they take a lot of work. It doesn't hurt that this time I'll get some eye candy along with the signing."

"Nothing wrong with that." I smiled, thinking back to my own eye candy.

"How's it going with Jacob?" she asked.

I let out a wistful sigh and nodded. "Pretty great. We've been talking on the phone a lot."

"Oh, I thought he was here."

"No. His dad fell, and he went home to help his parents."

"That's sweet."

I nodded and reached for a book that had a

beautiful cover.

"That's a good one." Charlotte eyed my selection.

"I need something to keep busy while I recover." I turned my attention back to my half-sister. "The doctor said I get to have a walking cast soon."

"That's exciting." Charlotte smiled, but I felt tension run between us.

"Okay, I'm going to just come out and say it."

Charlotte tucked a leg under her and nodded. "Please do."

"I really think you need to talk to Dad soon. The first few months that went by without telling him, I chalked it all up to nerves, and I dealt with it." I shook my head and shrugged. "But now it just feels plain wrong. If something were to happen to him, and he didn't know, I would feel awful. Not to mention, every time we talk on the phone, it's like this big cloud just hovers over us. I hate keeping secrets, especially from my dad. Anyway, it's not my news to share, but it does affect us all."

Charlotte's lips fell into a frown. "I know you're right, but every scenario I run in my head just turns into something awful."

I reached for her hands. "It's not an awful thing, Charlotte. It's a good thing. You're gaining a family."

She nodded. "I know. It's just that I feel like I'm betraying Mom because I promised I'd never tell."

"And how is that fair to you?" I smiled. "I know we're in a small town, and things were certainly different back in the day from how they are now, but you've already missed out on knowing your dad growing up."

"That's not entirely true," she said, twisting her fingers together and placing them on her lap. "That's one of the reasons I became friends with Vera. It gave me an excuse to get to know the man who fathered me."

"But that's just a glimpse of him."

I thought back to her statement and wondered about Vera. Did she know this?

"I know, and I promise that I will talk to him soon. I was actually planning a trip to Arizona. I don't want to do it over the phone."

I nodded in agreement. "I understand. Do you

want any of us there? I know we'd be more than happy to support you."

She shook her head. "No, I should do it by myself."

"Okay. I totally get it."

Charlotte smiled. "I don't want you to think I only became friends with Vera to find out about my dad."

I let out a sigh of relief. "I was kind of worried about that."

Charlotte laughed. "I know. I could see it all over your face."

I grinned and scooted to the back of the loveseat. "I'm really happy you're part of our family. First of all, you took Vera off our hands for a long time."

Charlotte snickered.

"And second of all, you're a really fun person to be around."

"I feel really lucky." Charlotte nodded. "And I want to believe my mom would understand my reasons for revealing our secret."

"I think she would."

Charlotte smiled just as my phone buzzed.

The moment I slid my phone on, my cheeks

blushed to an instant crimson. There, in all his glory, was Jacob Miller with nothing but a cowboy hat over his privates.

I couldn't help giggling as I stared at his beautiful physique.

"Never in a million years," I said, laughing.

"What?" Charlotte's right brow arched.

"Jacob just knows how to make me smile."

"I can see that." Charlotte grinned. "I really hope I find someone like that someday, but every year that goes by gets me a little worried."

I laughed and nodded. "I hear ya. I never thought it was in the cards for me, and then I went to a funeral."

"Ah, yes. The infamous funeral."

"I never would have guessed that going to pay my respects to someone who'd been a little shady in the past would open so many doors."

"Maybe it was his way of apologizing."

My eyes connected with Charlotte's, and I tilted my head.

"Hear me out," she said.

"I'm all ears."

"Well, what if the guy who passed felt awful about the wrongs in his life and wanted to make them right before he made his way to the other side?"

I smiled. "It's a lovely idea, but he wronged a lot more women than just me."

"I'm sure he did, but maybe you're the only one who would show up."

I liked how Charlotte thought and nodded. "You know what? I think you could be onto something. The whole trip felt like it was being orchestrated by someone else. The doors just opened right up, and I fell right into Jacob's life."

"Or he fell into yours," Charlotte suggested.

"Exactly." I grinned, sneaking another look at Jacob.

"Did he send you the kind of pic I only hear about?"

"Maybe," I confided.

"Then he must really trust you."

The words spun through me as I thought about Jacob. He made me feel incredible and worthy and excited for the unknown.

"He asked me to sing a duet with him. Actually, he asked if I wanted to record it."

"And you said yes, right?"

I shook my head. "It just seems like a big step."

Charlotte chuckled. "You've slept with the man. You think about him all the time. You can't wait to see him again. Yet, recording a song with him seems like a big step?"

I snorted at the absurdity. "You're right. Ever since I opened the doors to the universe, good things have come my way." I glanced at my foot. "Minus the breaking the ankle thing."

Charlotte smiled. "I'm so excited for you. Does he have any relatives?"

"He might. I haven't met any yet."

She chuckled as I thought about the decision I'd finally made. What was the worst that could happen?

The best was that it gave me a reason to surprise him. The moment he got home and I had my walking cast on, I'd fly out there and tell him the good news.

I had no idea what the future held or what I even

wanted out of life, but with Jacob by my side, it all seemed less daunting.

Samantha was right the other day. Was it really the thought of leaving Cloudberry that scared me, or was it more about the unknown that scared me?

All I knew was that it was time to find out.

CHAPTER TWENTY-SIX

Jacob

When I'd gotten off the plane in Montana, I immediately felt like I was home. Home wasn't a concept I'd ever gotten to know in my adult life, and I really liked the idea.

I also knew I had to see Lana again. She'd been on my mind the entire trip away, and I was pretty sure if my parents heard another word about her, they would have bought the engagement rings themselves, so I tried to restrain myself.

But the moment I pulled into the drive of my Montana home, my heart screeched to a halt. Never in a million years could I have planned for this. As I slowed down and pulled up slowly to my own home, I craned my neck to see a pile of luggage on my front porch.

A cold sweat swam over me as I took a deep breath and turned off the engine.

There was no sign of her, but her luggage was spread out all over. My stomach knotted as I climbed out of the truck and watched her walk around the corner from the patio out back.

Delila squealed and threw her arms up in the air. "I missed you so much."

She came running toward me, and it was as if every cell in my body had a visceral repulsion. She looked exactly like I'd left her in San Francisco.

Delila flew into my arms, but I didn't grab her or reach for her. Instead, I stepped back a couple of steps, shaking my head. She was left standing a foot in front of me, scowling.

"Has the Montana air made you forget about me?"

"Uh, Delila. I'm not sure why you're here. We both know you don't miss me. You don't even know me, but you did know and love my house in San Francisco."

She laughed and looked around the nature preserve around my home, glancing at the lake. "I'm sure I can get to know and love this place too. I can keep you company when you're not on the road and—"

I shook my head. "Not to going to happen, Delila."

She shot me a pouty look and crossed her arms over her chest. "You're not kicking me out, are you?"

I laughed and sighed. "How did you even find out about this place?"

"Your manager. He said I'd be good for you. That I'd help you gain perspective."

I chuckled, realizing Ted knew me better than I realized. Normally, having someone like Delila turn up on my doorstep was a quick method to get me back out touring again. I didn't have the heart to kick them out, so I left.

But not this time.

My main concern was Lana and persuading her to come to Montana for the rest of the summer, and if I were lucky, into the fall.

"I'll just be straight with you, Delila."

She shrugged as if honesty didn't matter to her one way or another and scanned the lake.

"I've met someone. She means a lot to me." I slid my hands into my pockets and watched Delila to see if any of this was resonating. "In fact, I'm inviting her to spend the rest of the summer with me."

Delila let out a deep sigh and frowned. "My Malibu place didn't work out."

I nodded. "I figured."

"They lived like animals." She shuddered. "Every picture I've posted since I got there makes me look angry."

"I'm sorry," I replied, doing my best to act as if I cared.

And in a way, I was sorry. She made a living posting lies to the world about her glamorous life. She needed good props.

"Posting from here would be amazing and totally unexpected." She grinned. "My followers would die."

"Geez. I hope not."

"Oh, I can just see it now. City girl turned country."

I shook my head. "I'm sorry, but I don't think my

girlfriend would be thrilled, and I wouldn't either, to be honest."

Her shoulders slouched, and she grunted. "Can I just get a few photos to post? I have to book my flight out of here anyway. I'll have plenty of time. I can crash in a guest room. Finding a flight will take some time."

"Not that much time. There are flights in and out of the airports all day. I can get you a car."

"Wow. You're serious."

I nodded. "I am. I think I'm falling in love."

Delila nodded, and for the first time ever, I saw a sweetness weave through her gaze. "I have a question for you."

"Okay. Go for it."

"Why did you let me stay at your house?" She laughed nervously. "I kind of felt like a glorified pet sitter, but you didn't have any pets."

"About that..."

She grinned. "I mean, we were intimate like once. Kind of. I kind of worried I was just your cover."

"But the photos at the house and the city were great," I teased.

She chuckled. "A girl's gotta do what a girl has gotta do."

I nodded, finally seeing the humanity from Delila I'd always wondered about.

"I didn't like coming home to an empty house."

"Even though you were never there?"

"Yeah, but... and no offense." I smiled. "The house still felt empty."

"What about this girl you're into?"

"She made me realize it wasn't the house. It was me. I was empty."

"Wow." Delila smiled and drew a deep breath. "That's beautiful. You should make it a song."

I laughed and nodded. "I just might."

Delila looked amused until the sound of a car came up the driveway.

I spun around, not expecting anyone, but I didn't expect Delila, either.

When I saw the shadows of a slender figure in the back of the car, I froze.

This didn't look good at all.

Not at all.

"It's not her, is it?" Delila asked. "You didn't tell me she was on her way."

"I didn't know."

"Oh, crap."

The car pulled slowly to a stop in front of us. Lana swung open the car door and started to hop out of the car as I got to her.

"Surprise," she said, stretching her arms for a hug.

"What a good surprise," I said, sweeping her into my arms, realizing she hadn't seen Delila or the pile of luggage yet.

We slowly broke apart as the driver lifted Lana's luggage out of the trunk.

"I hope it's okay that I—" She stopped talking when she noticed Delila standing on the porch next to her pile of luggage. "Did I interrupt something?"

"Not at all," I assured her.

She looked at Delila and then back at me. "I didn't know you had a visitor."

"She was a bit of a surprise to me as well." I let out a deep sigh as I watched the wheels spin in Lana's mind.

"Who is she?"

"She's a woman I knew before you."

"Was she your girlfriend?"

"I wouldn't call her that. No."

As if sensing some explanation was needed, Delila made her way over, which only made Lana stiffen.

"Hi." Delila stuck out her hand. "I'm Delila."

"I'm Lana."

"Nice to meet you. I've heard nothing but wonderful things about you." Delila grinned, glancing at me.

I thought things might just be okay.

"Really?" Lana asked, eyeing me.

"Oh, yeah. He wouldn't even let me stay here."

Lana's eyebrows arched. "Is that a first?"

Delila bit her bottom lip. "Well, I used to live with him in San Francisco, but he—"

It didn't take long enough for Delila to even finish her sentence for Lana to spin on her good foot and climb into the car.

The driver, somewhat following the turn of events, put her luggage back in the car and climbed inside.

"Damn it."

"I thought she would have known some of the story, at least." Delila shook her head as the driver backed out of the driveway. "What do we do?"

"*We* don't do anything. I know where she's going."

"Where?"

"The lodge."

"I'm coming with you."

"I don't think that's a good idea. I need to explain things to her." Seeing Lana leave was excruciating. I woke up this morning feeling like I could conquer the world. I couldn't wait to get back to Montana and invite the love of my life to spend at least the summer with me.

Delila rolled her eyes in exasperation as the car pulled away.

"And you think your telling a woman who you'd kept a kind of big secret from will believe you when you tell her, *no... she might have lived with me, but she means nothing."*

I groaned and shook my head. "I see your point."

"Good. Now, let's go track down your woman."

Delila followed me to my truck.

"She's gorgeous, by the way. I'd kill for her body."

I smiled and nodded. "She's incredible and perfect in every way."

"Just let me start the conversation."

Delila nodded. "As long as you don't screw it up."

"I'm not going to mess anything up." I turned on the road leading to the lodge and glanced at Delila. "Do you realize this is probably the most we've spoken since we've met?"

She laughed and nodded. "Which is why I felt like a pet sitter without a pet."

I spotted the car that had attempted to drop Lana off at my house.

"She wants to be found," Delila said, glancing at me. "Otherwise, she would have told the driver to take her back to the airport. There are hotels around there too."

"I hope you're right."

"Of course I'm right."

I found a place to park, and Delila immediately hopped out of the truck.

"How'd Lana hurt her leg?"

"She sang a song with me and broke it getting off the stage."

Delila chuckled. "She took the whole break a leg thing a little too seriously."

I smiled and nodded. "Something like that."

Images of Lana flashed through my mind like a hurricane thrashing around all the emotions that came with meeting her. I loved the way her smile lit up the entire room and how she made everyone around her feel better for just living. I loved how she cheered on all those singers in the bar and how she loved to love.

By the time I'd made it inside the lodge, I couldn't find her anywhere.

"Do you think she's in a room already?" Delila asked.

"No. I bet she's talking to an old friend."

Delila followed me toward the lounge where I

spotted Grey, and sure enough, Lana was sitting at the bar in front of him.

His gaze caught mine, and he tried to hide a smile.

As we walked up to their conversation, Grey could be heard saying, "I'm sure there's a logical explanation."

Delila couldn't help herself and continued, "And there is."

Lana spun around on the stool with her walking cast banging into the counter as our eyes met.

"I don't think there's any good reason to show up and see either an ex-girlfriend or current girlfriend either moving in or moving out for the summer." She scowled at me, which I knew shouldn't make me laugh, but it did. Lana was just so damn cute, and it told me that she felt the same way about me as I felt about her.

Delila piped up, "I'm not a girlfriend."

"Are you his housekeeper?"

"I might as well have been."

Not helping, Delila.

"Listen, there was never and never will be

anything between Jacob and me. We were friends, and I used his house for my social media while he was on the road."

Lana glanced at me before bringing her gaze back to Delila. "Have you two ever?"

Delila shook her head. "No, not really. Full confessional. We thought about it. We tried, but it didn't work out. It was a make-out session that had no sizzle."

That was a good summary. It was a pretty intense make-out session, but it really didn't lead anywhere that I cared to remember.

"When he told me he was selling the San Francisco house, I was relieved because I'd found what I thought to be an amazing place to stay in Malibu with a whole bunch of influencers. Needless to say, it didn't work out, and I thought I'd surprise Jacob because I knew he wouldn't be dating."

Lana cocked her head slightly.

"I figured he maybe wasn't into—"

Grey laughed and shook his head. "Celebrities, man."

"Oh, he's very into women."

I smiled and shook my head. "No, I'm very into you, Lana."

Delila smiled as if her work was done. "I'll call a car service and be out of your hair by tonight."

Lana smiled, looking a little sheepish. "Sorry for the drama. I should have just heard you out."

Delila laughed. "Heck no. If I'd come across what you did, there would have been hell to pay."

I ran my hands along Lana's back, and she smiled as Delila wandered out to the patio that overlooked the lake. No doubt, she wanted pictures.

"She's really pretty." Lana looked up at me.

"You know what she told me on the way over?"

"What? Who's the crazy lady we're chasing after?"

I laughed and shook my head. "No, she said you were beautiful, and she wished she had your body."

Her eyes widened, and she shook her head. "Nothing like a beanpole to entice others."

"None of that, Lana. You're absolutely perfect the way you are."

She smiled. "Thank you."

"And before all of this happened, I pulled up in my driveway to find an influencer scouting my house."

Lana interrupted and held up her hands. "Which, by the way, is all foreign to me."

I laughed and nodded. "The one thing I remember her telling me is that it's all about appearances. You can be absolutely miserable in your real life, but it's the influencer's job to pretend that everything in their world is perfect and they're having the best time of their lives."

Lana looked at me with her beautiful eyes and smiled. "Well, I'm not faking anything, and I can tell you that I'm having the best time of my life."

I nodded, feeling like the world was filling me up with the biggest gift, Lana's love.

"You know, before all this happened" —I cupped her hands in mine— "I was going to invite you out here for the rest of the summer."

"Yeah?" She smiled and waggled her brows. "Well, I have news for you too."

"Lemme have it."

"I want to sing the duet with you." She rested her hands on my chest and looked up at me. "But it will take me a lot of practice to get it right."

I looped my arms around her waist as she hopped off the chair. "Then it's good you're spending the summer with me."

CHAPTER TWENTY-SEVEN

Lana

"I love you, Jacob Miller, and there's not a darn thing you can do it about." I folded my arms over my chest and watched him slowly make his way to me in the lower garden of the inn. The weather was bordering on frigid, and not a leaf was to be had on any of the plants surrounding this little piece of paradise.

"Yeah? Well, I love you too, Lana Roberts." He smiled and stood in front of me.

His sexy grin undid me as I looked up at the stately inn and smiled.

It had always been my home. Yet, I was finally

going to leave this place. I promised myself and my sisters that I'd never look back. I was ready to explore the world and had the perfect partner by my side.

"You ready to see what it's like living out of a bus for four months?" He wove his fingers through mine and pulled me to him.

"I think I am." I looked dreamily into Jacob's gaze, wondering and waiting to see what life held. "I've been on my own for so long that I don't know if I'll play nice."

He nuzzled his nose into the crook of my neck as I felt him smile against my skin. "You were amazing to live with this summer."

I smiled as his gaze met mine. "Which turned to fall."

"Everything about you is a dream."

I nodded. "I feel like that too. It's like any moment, I'll wake up and poof, you'll be gone."

"It's going to be extremely hard to get rid of me."

"Music to my ears." I hummed.

"Well, it certainly isn't mine." He chuckled and rolled his eyes.

"I told you that I loved your music, your voice, everything... but the lyrics were sad."

"I have a lot of happy ones now."

I nodded, thinking how much life had changed in a matter of months. I'd recorded the duet with Jacob, and my world turned right side up and upside down, all with one hit. I'd never imagined I'd have the kind of money I now have sitting in my bank account.

But none of that mattered to me. What mattered was standing right in front of me, Jacob.

He knew officially parting ways with Cloudberry was going to be an adjustment. It was one thing to play and pretend in Montana all summer and fall, but quite another to pack up your things knowing you're never coming home.

Home.

I looked into Jacob's eyes and knew home was where he was.

"You know I love you, Lana." He drew a breath. "And I wanted to wait before asking you to marry me."

My eyes widened. "To marry you?"

He smiled. "There's no rush. I know it, but the

thought of having you next to me for eternity is pretty enticing."

I chuckled. "Are you sure about the eternity thing? What if I'm a dud and Earth is plenty?"

Jacob laughed and shook his head. "There will never be enough time with you. I always locked myself up in the tour bus, kind of like my own self-created hell, but with you by my side, I can't wait to really explore the cities we visit. You make heaven exist every single day I'm with you." He cupped his hands around my face as his gaze dropped to my mouth. "I'm so relieved you decided to take a chance on us."

"It's not much of a chance, Jacob. You make my world complete. I'm not scared to fail if you're there to catch me or make a fool out of myself or break a leg."

"Let's not try to repeat that." He grinned.

"Well, now that I know that your manager is just a sneaky little bugger who looks like my deceased high school first, I'll adjust my expectations."

"Do you believe that any of this was created by

something we aren't aware of?" Jacob asked, studying me.

I quickly nodded. "I don't believe any of this was a coincidence. I believe the people who've touched us here on earth, who are now up above, played a direct part in this disastrous start to a relationship. I mean, a funeral? I meet the love of my life at a funeral?" I shook my head. "It has my mom stamped all over it."

Jacob smiled. "I feel like Evie played a hand in all this too. She knew who I needed better than I did."

"Someone with a pulse, for starters," I teased, thinking back to Lars. "I still can't believe Lars had been saving so much money all those years."

"You just never know who can change the world in such big ways."

I nodded, thinking back to what Grey told us about Lars. He'd apparently saved every penny he'd earned, apart from splurging on drinks, and donated over a million dollars to the local Boys and Girls Club.

"It made me feel a lot better about life in general. When I was at the funeral, hearing people's snide comments and not seeing his family anywhere made my heart hurt. I also found it hard to believe Lars hadn't grown one iota as a person since high school, but I was very wrong."

"It's nice to be wrong," Jacob said softly, looking up at Cloudberry.

I nodded, looping my arms around his neck as the breeze picked up. "It is very nice." I let out a sigh. "I thought I'd be at Cloudberry forever."

"You can always come back," he offered.

"Something tells me it will only be to vacation."

"Nothing wrong with that."

Roaming clouds slowly inched over the blue sky, almost immediately dropping the temperature.

"I hate to bring it up, but we should probably get on the road."

I nodded as a sudden nervousness wound through me, but I pushed it down. I couldn't be scared about the unknown any longer. The unknown was what made life exciting.

He silenced my thoughts with a kiss, and all my worries slipped away before he broke away.

I'll let you have some privacy with your sisters. I'll

meet you on the bus."

"Thank you," I said, smiling as we walked up toward the inn where Samantha, Charlotte, and Vera were sitting in the kitchen.

"Oh, here comes our little rock star." Vera grinned. She'd finally stopped blushing every time Jacob stepped into a room, so that was progress. Drew didn't seem to mind or notice, but we sisters got a kick out of it.

Jacob leaned down and placed a kiss across my cheek. "See you in a little bit."

As he took off toward the hall, he stopped.

"Oh, wait."

I turned my attention back to him as he came back into the kitchen.

Before I knew what was happening, Jacob bent down on one knee and pulled a little box out of his pocket.

"When we're side by side, it feels like we can accomplish it all." He smiled. "You've made me remember what it's like to have fun and to enjoy the little things."

"Jacob..."

"I can't stand not being married to you for another minute. If you make me wait until the tour is over, fine. But I at least need to know you love me as much as I love you. I want our little family to grow with nothing but love surrounding us in Montana."

My hand slid to my belly, and I smiled, knowing I'd only just shared the big news with my sisters.

"Let me do what cowboys do and make this a little more official." He grinned, touching my belly with his hand. "I love you more than I knew possible, and I can't wait to see what the future holds, Lana Roberts. Songs write themselves when you're around me."

A lump appeared in my throat out of nowhere, and I couldn't help but nod before he'd even asked the question.

"Lana, will you make me the happiest man in the world? Will you marry me and spend eternity with—"

I squealed out a yes before he was even finished as my sisters shrieked with delight and hugged on top of Jacob and me. It was the best lovefest I'd ever experienced.

Jacob was laughing as he attempted to slip the ring on my finger, and my world spun into a maze of happiness. Finding the love of my life, having a hit song, being pregnant with the man I love, and now marriage.

It might have worked out a little backward in some people's view, but it worked out exactly how it was meant to be. I'd learned a lot about myself over the summer, the biggest revelation being that I still didn't know what I wanted to do until I found out I was pregnant.

That was when everything just came together and funneled down in a direction that told me I wanted to be a mom, and I couldn't wait to share this experience with the only man I've ever loved.

I turned to my sisters as Jacob held my hand. "Did you three know about this?"

"Maybe," Samantha said, laughing. "But all day had gone by, and I kind of thought he had cold feet."

Vera chuckled.

I rubbed my belly and smiled at Jacob. "I think it's

too late for any sort of frosty tootsies at this point."

"I do have one question, though," Vera said, stepping closer. "Will you be okay on a bus for the first trimester and a half?"

I nodded. "The doctor said it should be just fine. I might get a little queasy, but that hasn't happened yet."

"And I have no problem canceling the tour if there's even one little hiccup," Jacob said, and I shook my head.

"Nonsense. This is probably my one and only shot at touring with a bigshot like Jacob." I smiled. "I'm what you call a one-hit wonder."

Jacob shook his head. "Doubtful."

"Is it true this is your last tour for a while?" Vera asked Jacob.

He nodded and rubbed my shoulders. "For a long while. I'm ready to just enjoy life."

"I'm so happy for you two," Samantha gushed, giving me a kiss.

"I'm the luckiest guy in the world."

"You just keep that up, and we'll last for eternity."

I smiled as Jacob gave me a kiss before heading outside.

"I seriously can't believe you're headed on tour with your boyfriend and engaged." Vera shook her head. "Go big or go home, huh?"

"What can I say?" I gave my sisters all a big hug again and felt the love from each of them. "I should probably get going, or I'll never leave."

Samantha smiled and took a deep breath. "I'm so proud of you."

"We all are," Vera seconded as Charlotte nodded.

"You promise you'll come to the Seattle show? I know I'm only singing one song, but—"

"Like we'd miss it," Samantha said, shaking her head.

I wandered slowly down the hall and tried to memorize everything about the old inn until I got outside and saw my sisters wave from the window.

I finally realized that Cloudberry had been my partner all these years, my shelter and place to hide from the world, but I didn't want to hide any longer.

I looked at Cloudberry Inn and smiled, touching

the door my mom had painted blue for me so many years ago. The memories rushed through me at an unstoppable rate.

The good times, the bad times, and the in-between times.

I heard the tour bus start up, and I looked at the inn one more time.

"Leaving you was the hardest thing I did in my life until it became the easiest," I whispered to the inn as the memory of my mom standing at the door comforted me.

I knew it was finally time to make new memories and not be held hostage by the old ones.

BOOKS BY KARICE BOLTON

SUNSHINE BREAKFAST CLUB
DASH OF LOVE

MR. MISTAKE SERIES
MR. MISTAKE
MR. ACCIDENT
MR. WRONG
MR. RIGHT

ISLAND COUNTY SERIES
FINDING LOVE IN FORGOTTEN COVE
LOVE REDONE IN HIDDEN HARBOR
TANGLED LOVE ON PELICAN POINT
FOREVER LOVE ON FIREWEED ISLAND
TEMPTING LOVE ON HOLLY LANE
CHANCE AT LOVE ON MYSTIC BAY
IRRESISTIBLE LOVE AT SILVER FALLS
LUCKY IN LOVE ON HOUND ISLAND
MISTLETOE MISCHIEF
ACCIDENTAL LOVE ON MEADOW COVE LANE
DISCOVERING LOVE ON CRANBERRY LANE
CHRISTMAS ON FIREWEED
IMAGINING LOVE ON WILLOW ROAD
CHRISTMAS CRUSH ON FIREWEED

BEYOND LOVE SERIES
BEYOND CONTROL
BEYOND DOUBT

BEYOND REASON
BEYOND INTENT
BEYOND CHANCE
BEYOND PROMISE
BEYOND the MISTLETOE

CLOUDBERRY INN SERIES
IMAGINING YOU
REMEMBERING YOU
LEAVING YOU
LOVING YOU

SILVER RIDGE SERIES
A HAPPY TRUTH ABOUT LOVE
A LITTLE SECRET ABOUT LOVE
A FUNNY THING ABOUT LOVE
A SURPRISING FACT ABOUT LOVE
A SIMPLE WISH ABOUT LOVE

LUKE FLETCHER SERIES
HIDDEN SINS
BURIED SINS
REDEMPTION
MIA

BLOOD TORN DUET
BLOOD TORN
BLOOD CURSED

V MAFIA SERIES
BLAKE

DEVIN
JAXSON

THE WITCH AVENUE SERIES
LONELY SOULS
ALTERED SOULS
RELEASED SOULS
SHATTERED SOULS

THE WATCHERS TRILOGY
AWAKENING
LEGIONS
CATACLYSM
TAKEN NOVELLA (A Watchers Prequel)

AFTERWORLD SERIES
RecruitZ
AlibiZ
UprisingZ

Contact Karice

Don't forget to join Karice's newsletter by visiting her website at karicebolton.com and don't miss out on all the updates and sneak peeks by joining her Facebook Group (Karice Bolton Book Buzz).

To contact the author, please visit her online at www.karicebolton.com or via Twitter/Facebook/Pinterest @KariceBolton.

www.ingramcontent.com/pod-product-compliance
Lightning Source LLC
Chambersburg PA
CBHW030624250626
47154CB00006B/1911